KEYS TO THE HIGHWAY

HORROR STORIES WITH A THEME OF
BLOOD SOAKED ROADS
AND PEOPLE ON THEM...

Edited by Dorothy Davies

KEYS TO THE HIGHWAY

GRAVESTONE PRESS

CONTENTS

CONTENTS

Tailgate Vigilante

Carl Hughes

1

Just after three o'clock on a November morning and the country road was deserted apart from Shane McCloud's silver Barranca with the custom-built searchlight fitted to the rear. At the moment the light was switched off but Shane knew it wouldn't be long before he'd have reason to use it.

His digital speedometer recorded a steady fifty miles an hour, which he reckoned was plenty fast enough for anybody. Even the terminally stupid and those with egos the size of Jupiter didn't need more speed than that. But then, you always found somebody who acquainted velocity with machismo and that applied to certain women as much as it did to male inadequates. Shane regarded most other road users as psychotic beasts. Like lunatics, they didn't act rationally or conform to civilised norms. Their brains might as well have been encrusted with barnacles for all the sense that spewed out of them.

After a couple of minutes he spotted a set of distant headlights in his rear-view mirror. At first they appeared as mere pinpricks on the black velvet of night but they were getting closer. And much closer. As if he were standing still.

In a matter of seconds the following car had come up close behind, its headlights not properly adjusted so they dazzled. The vehicle approached within twelve feet of the Barranca's rear bumper, its driver attempting to intimidate Shane into going faster. Whatever speed he accelerated to wouldn't be enough for the dickhead behind. Sixty, seventy, eighty: not enough.

Shane slowed to forty miles an hour, giving the cretin an easy opportunity to overtake on the otherwise-deserted road. But this being the twenty-first century, when British motorists and police regarded overtaking as a blasphemy, the other driver didn't go past. Instead he or she (it was usually a he but by no means always) inched even closer. Nine feet behind now and the headlights hurting Shane's eyes.

He reached with his left hand to the switch that he'd installed beneath the dashboard and he flicked it down. Instantly, the searchlight on the back of the Barranca came on, illuminating the cab of the car behind.

The vehicle contained only the driver, a hirsute individual wearing wraparound night-vision glasses. Blinded by the searchlight, the ape blasted on his horn but didn't pull back. If Shane braked suddenly, the car would plough into the back of his Barranca.

'Okay Becci, this is for you,' Shane muttered as if talking to a ghost. He eased up on the accelerator. Thirty-five miles an hour; thirty; twenty-five. The other driver blasted on his horn and mouthed off.

With his speed down to fifteen, Shane braked and finally brought his Barranca to a halt, slewed across the road so there was no longer room for the moron to pass.

Skeins of cloud skittered across the gibbous moon like ragged wraiths, harried by a bitter wind that seemed to have abandoned the Arctic out of perverseness. The birches and pines that lined either side of the road were sheened with silver moonlight, the roadside verge dusted with a sugar coating of frost. A rabbit, bobtailed and nervous, bounded into the trees as Shane got out of the car. He was wearing a voluminous coat beneath which he'd concealed the only thing he would need.

The other driver flung open the door of his big Skoda and leaped out, screaming obscenities. He was aged somewhere in his late twenties, had a jungle of hair and a face like a melted waxwork. Ugly didn't begin to describe him. Shane knew that ugliness would soon be the least of this creature's problems.

'Why were you tailgating me, you arsehole with shit for brains?' Shane demanded.

The waxwork thing whipped off its night glasses and lumbered forward, fists clenched by its side. The man was built like a grizzly bear on steroids, eyes as inflamed and unwholesome as a festering wound. When he spoke, his words were thick, like glutinous porridge, probably manufactured by a vocabulary of fewer than two hundred words. *Dawdling bastard* was one of the things he shouted. *Fucking bollock twathead*. That was something else.

Shane stepped forward, produced a tyre iron from beneath his coat and smashed it into the obscene creature's face. The other man staggered backwards, howling, hands going up to his nose as

9

if to satisfy himself it hadn't come off. Shane raised the iron again and brought it down over and over, crushing the idiot's skull. Bone splintered, shattered, blood spurted, yellow matter rained out of the jerk's nose and what was left of his head as he slumped like a bunch of hairy rags to the road.

Not done yet, Shane delivered more blows to the corpse until what had been the man's head resembled a mangled pulp of papier-mâché. Breathing hard, powered by rage bottled up for too long, Shane then snatched from his pocket a pre-printed message that read *The Tailgate Vigilante says keep your distance – you've been warned*. He used a tacking pin to attach the message to the ignoramus's quilted jacket. Then, before any other vehicle could show up, he returned to his Barranca and scorched off.

Home was a semi on a blot of estate fastened to the fringes of an urban eyesore. Shane and Becci had put down a holding deposit two days after they announced their engagement and, during the summer that followed, they'd paid off the remainder of the deposit in instalments and worked together on decorating the place, planting shrubs and flowers, getting to know their neighbours. They'd married in October and moved into the house on their wedding night, as they couldn't afford a honeymoon in some exotic place. Neither of them was worried about the lack of a getaway romance beneath palm trees. They had each other and wanted nothing more. The rest of the world could go on living in a toxic swamp that was regularly topped up with cant, hypocrisy and sleaze. For Shane and Becci, life bore no burdens or kookie chemistry.

It was after four-fifteen in the morning when Shane reached this haven after dealing with the tailgater. Not wanting to alert his neighbours to the fact that he'd been out during the dead hours when they might reasonably have expected him to be asleep, he left the Barranca on his driveway and closed the car door as quietly as the lock allowed.

The house smelled of violets, which had been Becci's favourites. This perfume came from wax polish and an aerosol but Shane wasn't concerned about the absence of the real things. After all, it was the scent that reminded him of Becci. He didn't need to see dying plants in glass vases to ground his mind or preserve his memories.

He slumped into the three-seat sofa, the piece of furniture on which he and Becci used to cuddle and canoodle while watching the box. The carpet was pale blue, the walls papered in cream and white. Becci liked light colours and had scorned Shane when he said he'd prefer the walls to be orange: his favourite colour.

'I'd feel I was living in a tangerine world,' she'd teased. 'Leave the décor to me and you see about putting in a light fitting without electrocuting yourself.'

Happy days full of bliss and forever. Only, it hadn't been forever after all.

2

Shane and Becci were inseparable, as deeply devoted to each other as a couple of any age could be. Then one night, two weeks after being confirmed pregnant and on her way home from the hospital where she worked as staff nurse on a children's ward, Becci was taken from the world that she'd blessed with her so-special existence. Her innate goodness, gentleness, kindness were snatched from those sick children and from Shane in a moment of what he regarded as maniacal murder.

It was in lashing rain on Sheringham Road, the main thoroughfare through town, that Becci braked hard to avoid a German shepherd dog that bolted across her path. The dog had slipped the leash held by its frail and elderly owner and emerged like a streak of canine lightning from a side street. A lorry travelling behind Becci's ageing Fiesta ploughed into her car, pulverising the vehicle and crushing Becci beyond recognition, killing her outright. Witnesses said the lorry driver had been tailgating her, trying to intimidate her into going faster, flashing his headlights, revving his engine.

When the police arrived, they found the driver had been drinking and had also taken in a drug stronger than nicotine. As aggressive and repulsive as a Neanderthal after a lobotomy, he showed no remorse for the death he'd caused. He only wallowed in self-pity with complaints of an unhappy childhood at the hands of abusive parents and a delivery schedule that placed him under intolerable physical and emotional pressure.

In court he'd broken down, not for the life he'd swiped away but for his own pathetic deficiencies.

The previous convictions he had for wife-beating, racist attacks, arson and petty theft were not his fault but the result of the shitty hand he'd been dealt by life, he said.

On being sentenced to a derisory handful of years in jail, he'd smirked at Shane who was sitting in the public gallery and given the thumbs-up to the bleeding-heart barrister who'd represented him.

As far as the law was concerned, a rightful penalty had been imposed and with that, having lost the only meaningful presence in his life and their unborn child, Shane was meant to be satisfied. 'Life goes on,' said an unfeeling friend just a few weeks after the funeral.

Only, for Shane, life could never move on as it had been meant to.

3

At eight o'clock, just hours after carrying out his act of justice on that hairy tailgater in the Skoda, Shane had to get up and prepare for work. His job entailed travelling a segment of the county, taking orders from commercial firms for oil and other lubricants. This meant he covered up to sixty thousand miles a year on business and, though he once enjoyed his time on the road, using it to learn Spanish and French through the car CD player (a hobby he'd shared with Becci), he now found it an ordeal because of the increasing numbers of imbeciles who'd contracted the tailgating infection. Their intimidatory antics had always caused annoyance but since Becci's death, Shane had

13

developed a pathological aversion to anyone who approached within spitting distance of his car's rear bumper. He regarded them as no better than puréed shit.

Tired, dishevelled, unshaven, he turned on the TV set and tuned to the BBC News channel before leaving for work. The main item was about a jail riot apparently caused by the governor's clampdown on drug dealing. Then came the sob story he'd expected, about the hirsute idiot he'd despatched so comprehensively in the early hours. Police had cordoned off the road, the man's relatives had been informed and the reporter had it on good authority that the victim had been loved by all and sundry, had never harmed a soul and would give his last penny to any beggar that came calling.

'Yeah, and no doubt he doted on pussy cats and saw little old ladies across the road,' Shane sneered. He felt no compassion for the man; harboured no sympathy for the sort of individual who attempted to intimidate others into endangering their lives. He experienced only a deadening listlessness of the soul.

David the paperboy had just pushed a copy of the local *Gazette* through the letterbox. The paper, published too late to report on the Tailgate Vigilante, was as usual choked with parochial tripe about bring-and-buy sales, charity auctions and karaoke evenings in the town's pubs. Some of its columnists wrote like cranky grannies preaching homilies about the good old days, which apparently went down well with the readership; or so Shane gathered from the letters page. He'd kept up the newspaper deliveries only because the *Gazette* had been Becci's favourite paper. One of her colleagues at the hospital had been married to the night editor, whose name was listed with numerous others of editorial significance on page two. Shane found the list to be an impenetrable jungle of job titles. Maybe one day, when the wound of Becci's loss began to heal (as he'd been assured to his protesting mind that it would), he might cancel the paper and similarly end subscriptions to *Nursing Times*. For now, he imagined Becci perched on the sofa, her nose in the papers, reading out bits that she thought he'd find amusing.

Bitter didn't begin to describe the way he felt, even though he hated his rancour. He knew it to be terminally corrosive and it was alien to him. Until losing Becci he'd been optimistic, breezy, popular, as happy as a man could be without realising or acknowledging the blessings that had enriched his life. Part of him now yearned to move on, to allow Becci's memory to survive in the cherished sanctity she deserved; but there was a shadowed gulf in his soul that could never be bridged or filled with forgiveness. Bile gnawed at his nerves like a poisonous serpent, lay sourly fermenting in his stomach and wormed its way into his turbulent dreams.

He no longer had Becci but he now had a mission.

4

His next victim was a thirty-something imperious business type in a BMW. When he struck the woman with the tyre iron, her wheezing breath sounded like December wind whistling asthmatically through wooden slats. She succumbed quickly, crumpling to the country road and twitching in the spasmodic throes of death for only a few seconds. Afterwards, the night felt as quiet as the muffled space beneath a feather mattress. Shane remained with the corpse only long enough to pin his message to the tailgater's camel coat.

With that second killing, he knew he'd entered the country of the lost. Becci's death had deprived him of the solder of his heart, the glue of his soul and now his only embrace was for the lady called justice. It was all he had.

5

So began an assassination spree as Shane struck with abandon, always in the same manner. The news media salivated over the infamies and wheeled out so-called experts to analyse the psychological profile of the Tailgate Vigilante. As panic swept the land, newspapers recorded soaring sales while their journalists shed crocodile tears for the bereaved families. Grieving widows and inconsolable children had TV cameras thrust into their faces, neighbours relishing their moment of fame talked about the loss of good, decent people who'd never given a moment's cause for complaint.

Drivers were first warned by the police and motoring organisations not to venture out alone at night and certainly not to tailgate; but there were always those knuckleheads who believed themselves to be indestructible, who insisted on driving *their* way and damn what other road users thought.

The police set up a special task force that after many months appeared to be making no progress in tracing a killer who moved like a phantom through the rural nights. Questions were asked in Parliament, newspapers printed lurid supplements and after more than thirty killings by the Tailgate Vigilante, a law was passed expressly outlawing the act of tailgating. It became a criminal offence not to leave at least five seconds between vehicles.

Shane was heartened to read the letters sent to newspapers by nervous old ladies and gentlemen who welcomed the new law, saying it made them less fearful of venturing out in their cars. Previously, they'd stagnated at home rather than get behind the wheel and it was all due to the intimidation of other road users and the fear of road rage.

Vindicated but still grieving, Shane attempted to conjure an image of himself as a knight errant, a travelling righter of wrongs, but conscience is a strange animal that won't be coerced into erecting columns of rectitude where something less wholesome should stand. The thought of further killings held as much allure for him as a boil on the backside but he knew he could never stop, or at least not until Becci rested easy in her grave.

But there was the rub. He recognised that he was deluding himself. Becci would never have condoned murder. Her mission had been to preserve life, to cultivate wellbeing, goodness and forgiveness. Although not a churchgoer, someone who believed that Jesus the itinerant evangelist would have been incredulous to learn people worshipped him as a god two thousand years after his death, she'd espoused and practised what had become accepted as quintessential Christian virtues. She had embraced charity, goodwill and compassion and she'd loved those who wished her harm through either envy or spite. Meanwhile, some of the tailgaters whom Shane had despatched had, according to the press, been devout churchgoers and even acted as deacons, wardens and sidesmen. He knew they weren't even worthy of uttering Becci's name. But no, Becci wouldn't rest easy if she knew he had set about lionising her memory with a tyre iron.

6

Spring came late, the daffodils not appearing until April and trees coming into pink blossom only towards the back end of May. Shane no longer listened to his language CDs while travelling the county. The chummy voices, enunciating foreign words and phrases like finest crystal, reminded him too much of what he'd lost rather than what he'd once hoped to gain.

On the night of May the twenty-eighth he turned on the laptop computer in the boxroom, the tiny chamber that he and Becci had laughingly dubbed *The Office* and logged on to i-Own: the latest and most cultist social medium. It was time to claim the credit, if that was the correct word, from what ought to be a grateful world.

Writing under the pseudonym of Jasper Buckthorn, he described what he'd done to avenge the memory of the most precious being ever to grace the planet. He listed his tailgater conquests in chronological order, spewed contempt over their names, dismissed the tributes paid to them as spiky tripe, told his readers that the cretins had been as much use to the world as ladders without rungs and declared that by his actions he'd saved countless innocent lives.

He likened himself to great wartime generals who regarded the deaths of troops as the collateral they were willing to pay for the greater good, saving more lives overall. Those generals were subsequently fêted as national heroes, they received knighthoods from the monarch and were eventually awarded peerages. Shane told those reading his i-Own posting that he deserved the same recognition and maybe one day a grateful nation would reward him for what he'd so richly earned and warranted. But for now, in these prejudiced times, he must remain anonymous. That was why he was concealing his real name behind a pseudonym. He signed off as *the Tailgate Vigilante*.

Afterwards, feeling strangely empty, as if lacking a purpose in some stagnant existence, he sat back and stared at the pale-pink wall that Becci had painted with a roller one summer afternoon. No doubt those wartime generals experienced the same emptiness, the same lack of fulfilment in the face of triumph.

Ten minutes later, kneeling by the bed with clasped hands, he said, 'Tell me, Becci, from the spirit world, how best I can go on avenging what happened to you. If you think I should stop killing, just say so and I'll do something else – whatever you want.'

He climbed beneath the duvet, turned out the light and descended on a familiar escalator of sorrow into a torment of dreams.

Then, a little after four o'clock in the morning, he was awakened by a hammering at his front door.

Alarmed, he sat up in bed. Then came a thunderous crash as the door was battered down. Heavy footsteps came pounding up the stairs.

Calm and fiercely relieved, Shane knew then that the nation had come to pay its debt.

Skin Covered Concrete

Rickey Rivers Jr.

The yellow glow of day was bright through the living room. Bill sat staring at his image, a 'Wanted' poster reflection. That night led him down a path to a choice he decided was right at the time. He put his hands to his skin and dug fingers deep into the flesh. He started with his arms, went to his neck and up to his face. Everything after that night had seemed like a scene between the now and then, a false version of living.

He hated everything he dug into.

Yellow became orange, then a darker shade. It was night and Bill couldn't sleep. He heard noise in his head and was sweating like summer was trapped inside. He thought of pain, of painlessness, the blood marks in his flesh and the blood on the road.

Soon it was day. On his way to work, he drove past the office building. Work didn't matter, nothing did. He made it past city traffic and finally reached a straightaway. He was focused on nothing, a demon on the road. Trees flew past on both sides.

In his head he recalled the night, the lights, the lack of light and the sounds that haunted him. Everything was a blur. A transfer truck sped past the opposite lane. Bill gave it a glance, but only a glance. He wasn't afraid. In a way he wished the transfer truck had driven straight through his own car, splatter him on the road, but leave him alive. He was guilty, he knew that and he knew his job would eventually know too.

Bill clenched the steering wheel, his eyes bulging. He saw his own fingernail streaked image in the rear-view and laughed. Then he saw the road again.

Let me go, he thought, *let me go.*

He went on driving, or rather coasting, existing on the road without direction. There was no ending in sight, nothing but road and more roads. Straight to where? He didn't care. He felt heat. The radio switched itself on and off against static loud over shoddy speakers.

Let me go, he thought, *let me go.*

***

Bill woke up in a white room lying on an all-white bed above all-white sheets. All he could think is that someone must have saved him from a head-on collision or some other means of destruction. But why would anyone save him from anything? He wasn't worth saving.

He sat up and surveyed the room. It was picturesque, if done by a painter with limited vision. All-white everything, even the carpeting, which seemed to be fresh and new. The curtains, which were white, didn't seem to hide any light from outdoors or expose a hint of darkness. The curtains were so white they couldn't shade anything. When Bill stood to check them he saw no windows were there either, only an all-white wall. All of it was too clean to make any sense.

22

A sound turned his attention to the all-white television, there was an image on the screen: a bicycle. Bill recognized it. He turned away and went to the bed. He held his breath, closed his eyes and told himself he'd wake up back in his car. When he opened his eyes he was still in the room.

Bill turned to the still functioning television. The bicycle was covered in blood. Bill shook his head. The image on the television changed again. It revealed a man dragging the bicycle off to the side of the road and tossing it into a ditch.

The all-white telephone rang and Bill nearly jumped out of his scratched up skin. For a while he stared at the phone, hoping it would stop. The phone ring increased in decibels each time, as a threat awaiting an answer. The phone rang twelve times before the noise became too much for Bill to bear.

He answered.

The phone felt like he was clutching a toy, a small bit of cheap plastic. He said hello. The sound on the other end was a bicycle bell. It rang twice as a greeting. Bill hung up.

The all-white television took his attention again. There was another video. In this one a man dragged a child off to the side of the road and tossed him into a ditch. The man turned and locked eyes with Bill. This man had Bill's face without scars.

Bill turned away from the man and went to the all-white door. He opened it and looked out. There was a void, a void of indifference. The room seemed isolated from everything else, a box of whiteness in a pool of smog. He felt heat again. He

23

shut the door and went back to the bed. The all-white telephone rang and Bill fell to the floor.

"I know," he said. "I know what I did."

Now there was static on the all-white television. This morphed itself and as it morphed it made a noise. It rang out louder than the telephone. The sound of static surrounded him. Bill covered his ears and wept. With eyes on the television he saw the static breathe itself into the room and produce the figure of a child.

The child stood before Bill, a boy, unmoving. Bill was in awe, mouth agape.

"Forgive me," he said. "Forgive me."

From the boy's mouth was a sound of screeching car tires. Then there was a voice, a small soft voice. "I am not my mother."

Bill lost control of his eyes, they went this way, that. Tears fell on his now naked body.

The boy spoke again. "I am not my father."

Fire was calling and Bill stood up; a tongue of flame struck from below. Static quieted and the phone rang even louder. Bill moved himself to answer, his eyes focused on the figure.

"H-hello?"

"Bill, we've got a couple here looking for information. They want to speak to you."

Bill recognized the voice. It was Terry, a co-worker.

"Terry, help me! I don't know where I am."

"Bill, I'm putting the mother on now."

Bill felt his tears evaporating. The drops of salt became steam in the air. The boy of static stood near with the glare of a statue.

From the other end of the phone was a crying woman who spoke in words that seemed to crackle. "Where is… my son?"

Next was a man on the phone. Bill couldn't make out the words but he was angry, exhausted, hoarse. He sounded like he'd been crying and struggled to speak through smoke filled lungs.

Bill tried speaking but his voice snuffed itself out in his throat. His thoughts came out of his eyes like air escaping tires. Heat was around him now. He smelled the void outside the room. The walls were burning.

Days later a man's body was found on the side of the road. He had burned alive. His flesh had nail marks, described by some as resembling pictures a child would chalk on concrete.

Sliding Down the Night Road

Rie Sheridan Rose

Sliding down the Night Road
headlights plucking at the ghosts
staring with empty eyes
at the jive steel mass
with the rolling thunder wheels.

Nine Inch Nails croon from the radio
and click on the steering wheel –
the tenth gone with the
finger it rode in on for a
lost bet in a nameless town.

Black diamond eyes glitter
in the green dash light…
dreaming a madman's dreams.
Humming along to the radio
with an off-key-nails-on-chalk-board whine.

Everywhere nails…one kind or another,
like the coffin-nail dangling
from the rear-view mirror,
or the doornail in the Lucite shift knob.
Nailed to the Night Road…

…so he can't escape
and dream.

Hazy Miles

Olivia Arieti

Garrett needed a rest. He had been driving for hours, left home in the middle of the night and now the blazing sun was blurring his sight. The van was creaking like an old wagon and for sure, the hood would exhale smoke soon. The road was flanked by dry fields only, a rusty blanket wherever he looked; no houses, gas stations or cafés anywhere.

He had to reach the coast by the following morning, the ship was waiting to take him to his station; his leave was over. A friend would collect the van and keep it in his garage until he came back, if ever he would come back. The soldier had left no one behind, his parents were dead and his wife, Debra, had passed away years ago. Her death induced him to enlist. He didn't know exactly if it was rage, hate or sense of duty... Maybe, he simply wanted to get away. He would never recover, but that was personal, his own problem.

His shirt was sweaty, the air conditioner wasn't working and by now the heat was overwhelming both inside and outs. He was hungry and the surrounding aridity made him also dead thirsty. Had he missed a sign and ended on the road to hell? The incandescent sun and asphalt were only the prelude, perhaps.

With great relief, Garrett finally caught sight of a roadside café; enfolded in the high noon haze, a torn tent wavered above the entrance and he had to make his way through a cluster of fleas. The room was shabby but not dirty; a pretty young lady was sipping coffee at a table opposite his, at two others, some boisterous guys were drinking beer and smoking heavily, probably workers or farmers taking a break. Garrett wondered how they got there, only a yellow car was parked in front of the café and there were no factories or farms in the surroundings.

The sight of the vehicle upset him; Debra had been driving one of the same colour when the accident happened.

Fried eggs, bacon and milk helped him get back to his senses. The girl was staring at him, while the men didn't even turn round. The owner, certainly the cook and also the waiter, had disappeared into the kitchen.

The girl moved over to his table.

"I saw you getting out the van and wanted to ask you a favour, Sir."

"Garrett, Miss. Now tell me, what can I do for you."

She looked embarrassed. "I'm Maggie, and was on my way to Willsburg when my car broke down, that yellow dodge outside. The lady who runs this place said the only mechanic in the surroundings will be away for a few days and it would have been better if I managed to reach the city and come back with one myself."

Her blue eyes were fixed on his and her smile was warm. Somehow, she recalled his wife.

"I could pay for the petrol, if you take me with you."

"No problem, if you don't mind riding with a complete stranger," he chuckled.

Maggie's eyes twinkled happily, "I'm sorry to intrude like this, but I really can't stay."

"Just another cup of coffee and we'll go," he assured.

Sudden gusts whistled through the haze, clouds of dust rose around the building and the panes started shaking. Garrett feared the cafe would be swept away like a rickety house in a tornado.

"We're used to this," said the owner who had come back with more coffee. "Our spirits don't appreciate too much stillness, they've already enough in their graves."

Maggie and Garrett gazed at her inquiringly. "This was a furious battlefield once where more than a bloodbath occurred. Many soldiers were buried around here and it's said that at night time, winged demons fly above still looking for some damned soul."

"Quite chilling, indeed," muttered Garrett.

"Afterwards, a tavern was built here where the poor spirits used to dropped in."

"The soldiers, you mean?"

"Whoever, also those who lost their lives on this damned road."

Maggie went white, while Garrett was more than convinced the lady had watched or read too many horror stories.

"When a violent storm destroyed the place," she continued, "my old folks purchased this piece of land and opened the café for the wayfarers like you."

By the time Maggie and Garrett left, the improvised sand storm was over; the atmosphere appeared unreal, disturbing; a sandy carpet stretched before them while a grey dust had powdered the whole area.

Inexplicably, Garrett felt tense while his new travelling partner seemed comfortable in the old van, glad to be by his side.

She was heading to Willsburg to meet her ex. They had a great story, but it ended and now she wanted to find out if there was still a possibility…

"I've never stopped loving him," she said. Her eyes reddened and her lips were trembling.

"A long time has passed since I last saw him, this is my only chance, our only chance… but his feelings might have changed in the meantime."

Garrett couldn't understand how the guy might have fallen out of love with such an adorable girl. He liked her straightforwardness and in part felt her grief his own with the only difference that he had no more chances.

When he told her about his loss, her face darkened, the eyes lost the glitter that made it so pretty.

"Do you miss her?"

"Every single moment of my life," he said solemnly, as though making a vow.

Maggie smiled gently and looked out of the window.

The scenery hadn't changed, the same baked plains forgotten and forsaken by mankind; it was too sunny to appear ghastly, but it did. The opalescent mist had turned pearlescent and for a moment, he believed he was in heaven; at least he might see Debra again.

"How long will it take to Willsburg?"

"If nothing goes wrong, we'll get there by dawn."

The girl looked relieved, probably she thought the trip would have taken longer.

Garrett had been driving for quite a while when he felt a warm hand on his jeans. He turned round, surprised.

"Would you like to kiss me?" she whispered softly.

The good looking fellow was used to girls making advances, but didn't expect such a request from Maggie. It disappointed him.

"A kiss is cheaper than petrol, huh?" he sneered.

He shouldn't have said that, but it was too late to take it back.

"Don't be silly, it's just that I like you."

"What about your ex?"

"He'll understand."

Night had fallen upon them rather abruptly, a disquieting sharp contrast with the luminosity of the day, when Garrett pulled over in the parking area.

He took her in his arms and kissed her passionately, tenderly. She cuddled up to him as though willing to remain there forever, her eyes imploring him not to let her go.

"Do you want more?"

31

"No, no, that's enough," and withdrew from his embrace.

"You needed to be kissed and I'm sure you also need what usually follows."

Maggie gazed at him, uneasy, "I'm sorry, shouldn't have asked you, but you remind me of him…"

Garrett was unable to understand his passenger's strange behaviour. Perhaps *he* shouldn't have trusted taking a stranger on board.

"Whatever, I don't regret it," he said, "You're lovely and very gentle, he'll be happy to come back to you," and added, "He shouldn't have ever let you go."

"Sometimes you just can't help it," she replied sadly, "However, I won't make any pressure, I'll let him take all the time he needs."

"That's most reasonable, dear, and when he comes back, it will be forever, believe me."

His words pleased her.

For the first time he wondered if he could fall in love again. The kiss had stirred his senses so long dormant; he hadn't fallen for the girl by his side, but her warmth and sweetness made him long for someone to love and to be loved as well. A nostalgic sigh followed. Suddenly, he felt confused, alone, too alone… perhaps, he too, needed time to understand what he wanted.

While driving, Garrett cast a furtive glance at his partner who had dropped into a slumber. She looked as beautiful as a fairy or an angel; for sure, she was having a pleasant dream for her lips were curled in a slight smile and the expression was peaceful, just like a child that had fallen asleep after listening to her favourite bedtime story.

A big lorry flashed by. Its piercing horn blasted his ears and woke Maggie up.

"Good gracious, I must have slept for hours."

"Quite a few, dear, it's about dawn and we still have some way ahead of us."

"Oh no," she cried.

"I'm sorry, baby, but it's taking a bit longer than I thought, can't force this engine more or it will break down, just like yours."

Unexpectedly another roadside café appeared. Maggie asked him to stop.

"I'll go in and get some coffee for both and refresh a bit, just wait for me here."

She jumped off rather hurriedly, headed to the café and, before entering, turned round and smiled at him.

Garrett was already relishing the smell of hot coffee when, at the crack of dawn, the shrill cry of a cock resounded loudly. He looked around, but no fowl was in sight; probably, it came from the café's backyard.

The skyline quickly turned pink and a shimmering mist was about to veil the place. He began to worry. Why was it taking her so long? The best thing to do was to go inside.

The place was neat and clean, white curtains at the windows and white tablecloths on the few tables. It appeared new, as though nobody had ever stopped there.

The hoary guy behind the counter looked cadaverous, the face, emaciated and he was as thin

33

as if he hadn't eaten for months. His enormous candid apron seemed to cover a skeleton.

"Can I help you, Sir?"

"I want to know where's the lady that came in quite a few minutes ago."

The fellow gazed at him, dismayed, "What lady? No one has come here."

"She wanted two coffees and needed to refresh herself."

"I'm sorry, Sir, you can also check the restroom, but I assure you that nobody has entered this place."

By now Garrett was more vexed than worried; he rushed to the restroom and there was no sign of Maggie, then he went out and around the structure; the cock was there gazing at him, his black eyes twinkling sinisterly.

"I don't like these kinds of tricks, man, I'll go straight to the police if you don't tell me immediately where she is," he menaced once back in the café.

"Go on checking and you'll find out for yourself that there's no lady here."

Garrett was bewildered. What was going on? There was no reason why Maggie should have run away across the barren fields and risked to fall dead from a sunstroke.

"Here, have a cup of coffee, maybe you've been driving for long and are exhausted. This is an infernal highway, Sir, gelid and bleak in winter, burning as hell in summer."

Garrett pushed away the cup rudely and went out.

Could the driving and the heat really have driven him crazy or was it a trick of his imagination or worse, an hallucination? He didn't even know who Maggie was and she had dragged him into that absurd nightmare...

After waiting for a goodly long while, he got back into the van and drove out of the parking. He laughed like a madman on casting a quick glance in the driver's mirror; the café was no longer there. He had definitely gone mad.

Once at his destination, he would see a doctor immediately, tell him all about his encounter, the strange cafés and surely he would be put on pills.

That's exactly what happened and, while spending months at the hospital, he had all the time to realise that no girl could replace his beloved. Maggie's image flashed before him; her face was radiant and he noticed that the resemblance with his wife had grown more evident, the features were exactly hers.

Garrett's eyes filled with tears; no vision or hallucination occurred in that surreal trip... Debra had come back to him, eager to know if he still loved her...

When, on his first day back on the front a bullet pierced his heart, she was there waiting for him.

Roadside Assistance

Edward Ahern

Kristin almost ran over it, the sodden dark clothes blending into the wet asphalt. She swerved her car onto the far side shoulder, spun back onto the road and stopped with her headlights back facing the body. It hadn't moved.

Her first thought was to drive away. Someone else must have had hit him, but she'd be the one arrested if she stayed. She sat for several seconds; hands clenched on the steering wheel. Then, with the engine still running, headlights on, she got out of the car and walked through the frigid rain toward the lumpy shape.

It was a him. The upturned side of his face had a bleeding road rash. She could also see his shirt gently swelling and deflating, Alive then. She knelt and held his shoulders. His hands and feet were bound. As Kristin took out a pocket knife and cut the ropes he stirred. "Hey!" she yelled, "I'm going to call 911. You're hurt." *And I'm going to take off before they get here.*

He turned his head and opened his eyes. "No! No, I just got knocked out for a second." He tried to get up but his legs buckled and he dropped back down onto his knees. "No ambulance, no cops."

It was one AM, the two-lane county road had only rows of winter-bare trees as witnesses. The almost freezing rain spattered down. He tried to get up again, staggered and Kristin caught him by the arms. "You need more help than I can give you," she said.

His laugh was guttural. "Too true." He shook himself and stared. Kristin stared back. He was young, at least ten years younger than she was, muscle-bunched rather than skinny, maybe three inches taller than her 5'10". Good looking despite the dousing and scraping. "Is your car here?" she asked him and inwardly cringed, she'd have seen it if it was.

"No. No, no car. Look..." He reached into a pocket, pulled out a wad of bills and peeled off two hundreds. "I need a place to get cleaned up. Is there a motel anywhere around here? Could you take me? I'll pay you."

Not complaining about his injuries, so maybe not a scam. "There's nothing for the better part of fifty miles. My place is a couple miles further up. If you're okay I'll take you there and you can clean up."

He hesitated, seeming to calculate.

She added, "my dog will protect you from me."

He smiled; calculation complete. "Okay."

She helped him, limping badly, over and into her car, then pulled a blanket out of the back seat and handed it to him. "It's got dog hair on it, but it'll help you dry off."

"Thanks." He looked around as if he was expecting someone. 'The sooner we get away from here the happier I'll be."

"Got it. We're on our way. I'm Kristin, Kristin Hutchinson."

Brief hesitation. "Just call me Michael."

"Okay, just Michael." Kristin made a three-point turn and headed back east. "How the hell did you wind up there?"

"I rolled out of a moving car. Long story I don't want to tell you."

She glanced at him, nodded. "Okay. Cops after you?"

"I don't think so."

A half mile up the road an oncoming car roared by them, hogging the median and almost forcing Kristin onto the shoulder. "Asshole!" she yelled.

Michael had slumped down in his seat. "He is."

Kristin turned left onto a two-track dirt access road and drove a hundred yards in. Her darkened cabin squatted at the end. She turned to Michael. "Just sit here while I fire up the generator."

She walked over to a large shed and went in. A few minutes later the hoarse throbbing of a diesel generator kicked in and the porch light came on. Kirsten went back to the car, helped Michael out and put a hand under his arm to steady him as he walked up the steps/

Kristin called out, 'Heel, Alphonse."

Michael nodded. "So there really is a dog."

Kristin double unlocked the heavy oak door and went in first, turning on the lights, Michael following. A hundred-pound dog stared silently at him. It looked to be a Rottweiler/Pit Bull cross. The cabin had no feminine decorating touches, but was in inspection order.

"Why Alphonse?" Michael asked.

"As in the 1900's comic strip. Except what he does is never funny." Her expression was blank. "Never mind, just my weakness for the obscure."

She waved toward the bedroom. "Bathroom's inside there. The hot water's gas, so you can shower right away. My ex left some stuff in the closet he didn't want, you might find something to wear. I'll wait out here, brew some coffee. Unless you'd rather have a drink."

"Thanks. Booze please." He limped slowly into the bedroom and shut the door. After a few minutes Kristin heard the gas boiler fire up. A half hour later he came back out, wearing paint-stained jeans that were too loose and a Harley-Davidson Tee shirt that was one size too small. His scraped cheek was raw and red.

Alphonse had already been let out, let back in and fed and now sat at Kirstin's feet. His eyes never left Michael.

Kirstin handed him a double shot of bourbon in a water glass. "Sorry, the ice isn't frozen yet."

He downed a shot's worth and began to sip. "That's okay, I don't need nice." He settled gingerly into a padded Adirondack chair. "You don't look worried, didn't argue for calling the cops. Living off grid like this maybe you don't want to?"

Kristin shrugged. "I've been on the down low for a while."

"I need to ask a big favor of you. But I'll pay for it."

She said nothing, waiting for him to make his play.

"I need to borrow your car."

Kirstin's laugh was window-cracking. "I know it's a beater, but it's the only car I've got. Sorry."

His expression went flat, his tone even flatter. "You need to be rid of me quick, before trouble shows up. The guy driving that car has realized that I left with something of his."

Kristin dropped her polite smile. "Why didn't he just grab you when you rolled out?"

"Figured somebody was behind him. Couldn't stop."

"And now?"

"He needs what I have."

She chewed her lip. "Not likely he'll find us."

Michael shook his head sideways. "That was his car that almost ran you off the road. He's seen that I've not where I fell out and probably remembers your car. Country setting like this, he'll ask two or three farmers and learn where you live." Michael's lips tightened. "George has a gun."

He tried to cross his legs and failed, wincing. "I can give you two thousand now and arrange to pay you another five thousand. When George shows up you tell him I stole the car."

Kristin said nothing for several seconds. Then, "You can't walk, can barely drive. I'll take the two thousand, but I'll drive you to the airport. Once you're through security you can relax."

She considered. "His best play would be to wait for us to come back and Alphonse doesn't like unannounced guests."

"He'll shoot your dog."

"Maybe. But Alphonse has been trained not to bark before he bites."

40

The rain had stopped beating on the roof. The night had chilled further and frost was beginning to form on the windows. Kristin looked sourly at them. "They don't salt the roads around here and black ice is forming up. If we leave now, we're apt to go into a ditch before we get two miles away. It's your money, but we have a better chance of making it a couple hours after daybreak tomorrow."

The whiskey had reddened Michael's face, which remained without expression. He nodded. "Scary dog you've got, but I hope you've also got a rifle or a shotgun. Or you can just take the money and loan me the car. George will figure I'm gone when he sees you're still here but your car isn't."

Kristin waved a dismissive hand. "You'll wreck my car and I need quick transportation as badly as you do. We're going to have to rely on Alphonse and a twelve gauge until morning."

She sipped her whiskey and thought. "If he's willing to kill us, you guys didn't just knock off a convenience store. I should ask for more money."

"Two grand is all I have on me. I'll make it ten grand later."

Her smile was wry. "And I should rely on honor among thieves?"

"It's the best I can offer."

His glance measured the distance between them. He outweighed her by fifty pounds, but with his maybe busted leg he had no chance of getting to her. "Okay. Tomorrow morning."

Kristin stood up. "No supper, I can't be preoccupied with cooking. Pull the curtains shut in the bedroom, sleep on the floor next to the bed, not in it. I'll sleep out here. Put the money on the table before you go in."

Michael smiled. "You sound like you've done this before. Okay." He pushed himself up from the low chair, almost toppling over when his hands left the armrests. "Damn, that hurts." He counted out two thousand in hundred-dollar bills and put it on the table, stuffing a few bills back into his pocket. Then he shuffled into the bedroom and shut the door.

Alphonse hadn't moved during their conversation. "Watch," Kristin ordered, then went outside into the cold, dropped her pants and pissed into the frozen weeds. Once she returned, she pulled the Remington semi-auto from its case and loaded five deer slug rounds into it. Then she slewed the heavy sofa around so it was between the bedroom and the door and windows, pulled the curtains shut, cut the lights and lay down behind the sofa.

She woke when Alphonse growled softly into her ear. Two minutes later there was a loud knock at the door, followed by a shout. "Open up, bitch. I know you've got Roger in there."

Kristin took a shooter's kneeling stance behind the sofa and aimed the shotgun at the door. "Beat it before I call the cops."

Michael/ Roger tottered out of the bedroom. Kristin waved him back and hissed, "Lay down before you get your ass shot."

There was a laugh from outside. "No phone line, no cell service, you're not calling anyone. And I seen the dog shit on the grass. I'll kill it first."

"Good luck breaking into a dark cabin and not getting shot."

George banged on the door. "I'll burn you out."

Kristin snorted. "Cabins covered in ice. Might take a couple days."

Two minutes of silence. Then, "All right, tell Roger to open the door and throw the thumb drive out onto the porch. I get it, I'll go away."

Michael/Roger had crawled up behind her. He whispered," No way, he'd have to check it and make sure. There's no iPad or lap top in his car."

Kristin waved him into silence, then yelled. "We're going to talk about it."

"Don't talk too long."

Kristin turned to Michael/Roger. "How the hell did you get hold of his thumb drive?"

"His duffel bag was with me in the back seat. I came to while he was busy dodging traffic, unzipped the bag and got hold of the drive."

"Okay. Is it Michael or Roger?"

A pause. "Roger."

"Okay, Roger, here's what you're going to do. You crawl back into the bedroom, pull yourself up on the rear window sill and open the window. Then get out of the way."

"Hah?"

"Just do it. Fast as you can crawl."

Roger scuttled toward the bedroom whilst Kristin tiptoed to the front door. Alphonse moved with her. She waited a half minute, then knelt down to his floppy ear. "Window," she commanded.

Alphonse ran toward the bedroom, nails skittering on the wood floor, then jumped through the window. As he did so, Kristin loudly turned back the bolt on the first door lock. George immediately slammed into the door, but the dead bolt held. Kristin waited two beats, slid back the dead bolt, whipped open the door and jumped to the side with it. George fired twice into the room, then screamed.

Kristin spun into the doorway and fired a deer slug into George's right hip. "Heel," she yelled.

Alphonse released George's neck and Kristin fired a second slug, taking off a significant chunk of George's head. Roger hobbled out behind her. "Jesus," he said, "Jesus."

Kristin picked up George's gun and stuck it under her belt. "If you're going to puke, do it outside." Then she went through George's pockets and retrieved a car fob. She turned to Roger. "Wait here. I'm going to go find his car." She turned to Alphonse. "Watch."

It took fifteen minutes, but she drove the car, sliding, up the drive. She parked and walked toward the porch, where Roger was waiting, wearing her ex's winter jacket.

He raised his right hand. It held a small, concealed carry automatic. He smiled. "George's ankle gun. My turn to give directions. You know, funny thing about guys, even if they storm off, they usually take their shaving stuff with them. But your ex's razor and shave cream were still in the bathroom. And the bedroom had what looked like all his winter clothes. Funny."

Kristin stayed silent, so Roger continued. "Figure if you can off your partner you could off a total stranger. So, what should I do with you?"

She took out her pocket knife, opened it, then glanced at the dog. "Alphonse, ready." The dog's muscles bunched.

"It's the same deal, Roger, except you get George's car and can drive yourself. If you're able to kill me and the dog you've got three bodies to dispose of in frozen ground and a whole lot of your DNA strewed around the cabin. You can barely stand up. Figure it out."

Roger's grin was con-man winsome. "You are good." He lowered the gun. "Okay, truce. While I've got the gun, why don't you walk me to the car. You give me the fob and I'll be gone."

"Okay. Hold onto me harder than you do the gun. It's slippery. Alphonse, heel."

She carefully frog-walked Roger over to the car and helped him in, the dog padding next to his gun hand. He started the engine and looked up at her. "You never asked about the thumb drive."

"It's better that I don't know. Less need for you to come back and see me sometime."

"Yeah. You probably shouldn't expect that I'll be sending you money."

"I don't. "She patted the side of the car as he put the car in gear. "Don't bother looking for the fifteen thousand in George's bag. It disappeared."

The Haunted Lane

Stuart Holland

"Haunted Lane? Don't be daft, Mum. There's no such thing."

"Trust me, dear, there is. It exists by name on the edge of Clarewell Village. It's a long, windy road that leads mainly to large, derelict houses. I think the name's well suited to the surrounding properties."

"You're joking."

"No, Steph, I'm not joking. For good reason. Your father went down that damned lane when you were fifteen. Six months later he died from cancer, as you know well."

"Yes, never forget it. But that must be a coincidence."

"Was it? There's a lot of rumours of bad things happening to people who drive down there at night." Maxine was weary, weary of her daughter never seeing her side of things.

"Oh well, you only live once."

"True. All I'm asking is, be careful when you drive over to Mark's this evening. Be careful to avoid that village and that road, especially after dark."

"All right, Mumsie, just for you, I'll be careful." Steph was now nineteen and had been driving for over a year, without a scratch on her little Ford Ka. She kissed her mother on the forehead and with a "see you later" she was gone. Literally.

It was eleven o'clock that evening when the doorbell rang. Maxine had been worried for over an hour. Her daughter always let her know when she was going to be out after ten, but there had been no SMS message or call. It was unusual. It was unsettling.

"Mrs Cavanagh?" The two police officers, one female, did not need to say much. Maxine slumped in the hallway.

"Yes," she said in a frightened voice.

"Can we come in for a minute, please?" The female officer was gentle, almost kind.

"Of course."

The front door was shut and the three of them went in the lounge.

"You may want to sit down," said the officer. Maxine took up the offer.

"What is it?" she said slowly, though she'd already figured it was not good news.

"You have a daughter, Stephanie Cavanagh?"

"Y… yes. What is it?"

"I'm afraid there's been an accident."

"Is Steph all right?" Maxine dreaded the inevitable reply.

"No, I'm afraid she's seriously injured. We're to take you to the hospital."

"What happened?"

"A tree landed on her car as she was passing under it. It looks like she saw it just as it happened,

47

there are skid marks leading to where the car came to a halt."

"Was she alone?"

"No, I'm afraid not. The passenger was not so fortunate," the officer said gently. "We have other officers going round to his parents to break the bad news. Now, if we can get moving… the paramedics said we had to be quick."

"One final question while I put my shoes on," Maxine had gone into the hallway, quickly put on her coat and shoes and grabbed her handbag. "Where was the accident?"

"Clarewell Village, little winding road called Haunted Lane. Quite extraordinary as there are hardly any trees near the road. This one just snapped off for no apparent reason, I'm sorry to say." Finally the male officer who wore the stripes of a Sergeant joined in the conversation.

"Oh, there was a reason. I told Steph to avoid that lane earlier this evening but as with many a teenager, she chose to ignore me."

"Why did you warn her about the lane?"

"Four years ago her father drove down there one dark evening and came home feeling, shall we say, strange. At the time he said it was as if he had been cut through by a ghost. I laughed at him but a few days later he went to see the doctor and was diagnosed with lung cancer, though he had never smoked. He died six months later. It was then someone mentioned that lane is said to be haunted. Tonight it's almost as if someone or something confirmed that. What's down there I have no idea and I don't really want to know. But there are others

48

in villages round here who say it's haunted and bad things happen to people who go down there after dark."

"Well, Mrs Cavanagh, you know a lot more about that lane than we do. Now if you're ready…"

Three hours later, at thirteen minutes past three in the morning, Steph died. It would eventually be recorded as brain trauma, caused by misadventure.

Six months later, Maxine plucked up courage and went to the scene of the accident. It was a lovely, clear crisp autumnal day. She looked at what remained of the tree and felt a cold breeze blow across her face. It was as if the wind was speaking to her.

"You're right to be afraid. Be very afraid. See the new sapling growing from the ground. In time it will cause another death."

Maxine whirled round but no one was near her.

"Hear my words, they are just and true. You will see."

"No, no there won't…"

She leaned down and saw the little sapling sprouting from the ground close to where the bigger tree had once grown. Maxine pulled until the young, tender roots yielded to the ground and the sapling came up in her hand.

"No sapling, no more deaths," she said softly to herself. It was then the wind groaned, as if in pain.

"I said, no sapling, no more deaths." Maxine spoke more loudly, more defiantly.

She crushed the tiny plant in her hands, breaking its stem and bending it in half before throwing it into the road. She turned and walked away from the tragic scene, the place where her one and only daughter died, vowing never to go down that lane again.

Her wish was fulfilled. A car behind her sounded its horn. The sound got louder and louder until Maxine felt the dull thud as the car rammed into her back. She was tossed forward and up onto the bonnet, before being thrown onto the road, crashing her skull on the tarmac with alarming force.

Just as she landed she saw, out of the corner of her eye, a familiar, but impossible being.

"Steph?"

"Mummy!"

The sound of the car disappeared in the same instant as the life force left the broken woman. A short distance away, a sapling poked the first shoot of new growth through the earth.

Behind the Mask

Rie Sheridan Rose

His eyes fluttered open, and a slow, sleepy smile crept over his face. Today... today was the day. He'd been waiting for this day for so very long now. He stretched like a cat, feeling every muscle elongate and pop. He had to be ready. He had to be focused.

He got to his feet, slunk to the closet and pulled open the door. He stood, head cocked, evaluating all the choices. Black, black, or black. How about black?

A nod of affirmation and he reached to take his favorite shirt from the closet. Three-quarter sleeves slashed in even, precise rows; collar removed; a tribute to Brandon Lee in *The Crow*, though not a copy of the costume. He pulled it over his head. Skinned into his leather pants—like stepping into butter. Finished off the ensemble with black combat boots that had seen better days. He studied the effect in the mirror. The smile seeped back onto his face. He looked creepy. Cool.

He went back to the bed, reached under the mattress and slid out the six inch knife he had stashed there. He tested the edge on the ball of his thumb. A fine line of red bloomed like a flower. Nice.

He sucked on his thumb until the blood stopped flowing, then made up the bed with hospital precision. One last time. Making things neat. He liked neat. Mostly.

He crossed to the door. Eased it open and listened. All was quiet. The rest of the house was still sleeping. Good, it would make things easier.

One wall of the room was covered in masks. Kabuki, hockey, Halloween, Hollywood replica... he had collected masks as fervently as a child might the latest cartoon animals. He ran his finger along them now. Which should he choose? What was appropriate for an occasion such as this? The hockey mask was so cliché. So was the Scream. Ah! Here was a fitting choice. A smooth white Kabuki face, minimal in detail, but with a single blue tear coursing down the porcelain cheek. Ironic.

He slipped the mask over his head. It felt good there. He looked in the mirror again. Smooth, white, emotionless—perfect.

He was ready.

In the hallway he trailed a finger over the family photographs hanging on the wall. Beautiful Caroline, apple of her Daddy's eye...hoorah, hoorah. Outgoing Steve, Mama's darling...ready, set, hup. One small photo of him... nobody's baby. Marilyn and Steve Sr., parental units in name only.

He came to the first door. *Sweeeet Caroline*, he heard Neil Diamond crooning in his head. Well, she'd never been sweet to him. She'd been a bitch from the first moment he could remember her. She'd pushed him down the porch steps when he was three, making him break his arm in two places. She'd told his first crush he had VD... he was twelve. Goodbye, Caroline...

He opened the door silently. He'd oiled every hinge in the house while the family was at the club yesterday—they'd never even considered his presence at the outing.

She was fast asleep. After all, school was four hours away and she was never one for early rising. Her blond hair spread like golden wire linking her head to the pillow... plugged in for dreamtime. She was a pretty thing, as meatbags went. He had to give her that. Perhaps he should add her face to his wall when he was done. Except there would be no wall when he was done.

When he was done, he would never look back. He would walk away against a wall of flames. Just like the movies. He felt a surge in his loins and looked down. A rather impressive bulge in his leather crotch. The slow smile crept back over his face. What to do... what to do?

No. She wasn't worth it.

He lifted the knife, placing one knee on the bed beside her. The mattress sunk under his weight and she shifted. His free hand snaked out fast as lightning and covered her mouth.

Caroline's eyes flashed open. There was terror in those blue eyes. It warmed his heart.

Though not as much as the blood that jetted from her throat as he slashed it. He would have howled in ecstasy, but the others might hear. There would be time enough for celebration when the work was done.

The fountain died to a trickle and he climbed off the bed, panting with release. The white walls now wore Pollack spatters of red shading to brown. And Caroline was the centerpiece of the painting.

He had a thought... and pulled his phone out of his pocket. Memories could fade. Photos were forever... or until the battery died. He snapped several shots from various angles. This would be the best family album ever.

Across the hall, Steve's bastion to football... plaid wallpaper and a trophy case covering an entire wall. The room projected cold. As cold as Steve's fucking heart.

He didn't waste time standing over his brother as he had his sister. A quick slash of the knife... photographs... and out. Steve was worth no more of his time.

He left the door open. By the time he was done, no one would mind the mess.

He strolled on down the hall, his boots marking his progress in blood. He began to hum under his breath, his favorite song, the genesis of his current agenda...

Ah, Mother and Father... parental units, at least in name... though they would deny it if they could. They slept together in their king-sized bed, entwined as if they were still young lovers, though they fought like dogs awake.

He stood over them for a moment. Steve Sr's hair was going gray and thinning at the top. It made him look old and... diminished. The killer smiled.

His knife swiftly drawn across his father's throat. The expected fountain washed Marilyn in red. The heated shower startled her awake and she wiped her hand across her face. When it came away red, she scrambled to a sitting position.

"What the hell?" she screeched. She stared around her wildly and when she saw Steve's second mouth, her scream could have shattered glass.

"Relax, Mother," he whispered from his place on the bed, a knee either side of her. "No one will hear you scream."

"What are you doing?" Even *in extremis* she didn't use his name. He noticed. Oh yes, he noticed.

"I want to fuck you, Mother." He grabbed her wrists. "Won't that be fun?"

And it was. So much so that he flipped her over and did it again. As his cock spasmed the second time, he slashed her throat, like all the others. It was much more satisfying than the orgasm.

When he was done, he stepped into the master bathroom and turned the gilt handles on the walk in shower. The rain shower sprang to life, cascading ribbons of water from dozens of nozzles. When it was warm to the touch, he walked into the spray fully clothed. He lifted his masked face to the spray and let it wash away the blood, and with it, all that remained of 'family' in his mind.

When he was relatively clean, he went to the living room bar—his father's pride and joy—and poured himself a stiff drink of his father's best. He slugged it down, grimacing at the taste, then grabbed the bottle and threw it against the stone hearth. The remaining liquid splashed onto the Persian rug. He emptied the other bottles on the bar, one in each kill room—taking pleasure with anointing each corpse—one in the kitchen, others

55

through the hall, until the air was redolent with the sharp scent of liquor.

He stepped outside the front door... and then dashed back in, ducked into Caroline's room and ran a finger through the congealing blood at her throat. He slipped the mask off his head at last—and drew a rose upon its cheek with the gore. Something to remember them by.

He left the house for the last time, pulling his father's fancy gold lighter from his pocket and flipping it open. He stared at the flame, a smile tugging his lips and then tossed it into the hall.

The flame guttered and then caught the pool of alcohol and burgeoned into a spread of fire. It was greedy... soon climbing the walls and licking at the photographs. When he was sure it had well and truly caught, he turned his back on it, reached into the bushes for the bag he had stashed there the night before and started for the road. He had a mind to see the world.

Road Rage

Dorothy Davies

Roads.

Hate them. Damn things just lie there on the ground, stretched out like pieces of black rubber bands or strips cut from tyres and laid there, held down with kerb stones each side or yellow lines or even, heaven forbid, grass because no one goes along there and cuts it, do they? Now why don't I think that a road with a grass edge is a real road?

What does it matter? I still hate them.

Well, listen up and I'll tell you why.

Cos the damn things go *somewhere* and *somewhere* ain't where I wanna go. Not any more, anyway.

Had the wanderlust, I did, itchy feet and all. Remember that silly song 'I was born under a wandering star'? That was me. Wanted to walk the world, I did, I saw what it looked like in China, Malaysia, Peru, any of them African countries, any of them A-rab countries, wanted to see what made the Arctic different from the Antarctic or were the road signs the same in both places, thick with ice and covered in snow and unreadable...

Joke.

Sorry.

Anyway – got the picture? Wandering me? Left the family a long, long time back, 'cos they didn't want to go wandering, they wanted to sit by the fireside with the dog and the cat and the vegetables in the garden and the thatched roof full of birds and twitters and creepy things that rustled the strands at night and scared the **** out of me. They're welcome to it, I thought, being all of seventeen, all growed up and knowing what I wanted. I thought.

Surprising how wrong you can be, ain't it?

So what I did for a while was, went walking miles and miles, sleeping by roadsides, ear to the ground, hearing the thrum of the lorries, oh man, you could hear them coming for miles, them great wheels pounding the surface and shaking the earth and then going by with a roar and a whoooooosh of wind so sharp and hard it could have you clean off your feet. And gone on to the next village, next town, next city. How come I never stuck out a thumb and got me a ride is the question I am busy asking right now. With no answer, unless it be that I needed to walk it myself, every step, even when dogged tired and feet so sore they could hardly stand the weight of me anymore. Talking of that, I lost so much weight I looked like a wraith, or so me Ma said when I went back. Least, I think she said wraith, she might have said rake, come to think on it. Not that it matters, either way I was as thin as one of them reeds thatching our cottage. And come to think on it again, I was fit to rustle like one of them, too, when –

But I ain't there yet.

I'm here. Like here. On the side of the road. Learning to live with the sound of the cars and the lorries and learning which was which, even by the engine and the thrum of the wheels. Oh my, I do like that expression, don't I?

You see, I never learned much in my life up to then, so I set myself the job of learning the difference and it worked and it felt good and I thought – hey, I can do sommat now that perhaps no other person can do! Oh that felt good. I mean, I ain't much good otherwise, am I?

What?

You know that song, "King Of The Road", yes, another song, grew up with songs, could tell you a hundred songs that fit this story, "Road To Hell" is one ... no, that old king of the road song, where he sweeps a floor and things like that. That was me. That was me labouring here and there, fix a gate for someone, muck out the stables for someone else, chop firewood, pluck a chicken, you be surprised how many people want sommat done if you just ask right and don't ask for money. I never did ask for money, never had any either. I got food and a night's shelter and sometimes someone took pity on me and would give me fresh jeans or shirt or a jacket that had a tear here or there but was just fine by me. Oh and a hat to keep the sun off. Suited me just fine.

I did that for what seemed like forever. Enjoyed it no end. Met all sorts of people, learned the good from the bad from the indifferent and the downright mean.

Then I met him.

Hold on. That should be Him.

I was walking this road, see, leaving the lorries and trucks and hauliers to themselves for a while, travelling a back road to see what it felt like. Different, I gotta give you that. Saw a fox or two, all sorts of scurrying things – didn't know what they were, what's the difference between a shrew and a dormouse and a field mouse and a –

Anyway, wild flowers and wild animals and good sunshine and then I realised, in a moment, that someone was walking with me.

There was no one there a breath before, I swear on my reputation, such as it be, as an honest individual. Then he was there. Dark face, dark eyes, dark thoughts and all.

"Do you mind if I share your journey?"

Like he was dressed for it, mind. Sharp suit and white shirt, blue tie crossed with gold lines, smart as you like, complete with polished lace up shoes. Not your usual kit for tramping the road, is it?

But I was brought up proper and even if I had a pretty cute idea of who he was, I said, nice as you like: "You're most welcome."

He hardly seemed to draw breath, was busy talking to me about roads, how they went somewhere and that somewhere was usually more interesting, or so we thought, than the place we had just left, when in truth all places were the same.

"No, they're not," I said when he paused for a moment in his discourse. "The people may look the same, but they ain't."

"Interchangeable, my friend, that's what they are." Then he stopped and looked at me. "You know who I am, don't you?"

"I do."

60

"And you haven't asked me for anything."

"Why should I? Got all I want outta life."

He frowned. "This isn't right. Everyone wants something."

"I don't."

"Not fame, wealth, women?"

Laughter consumed me for a moment. "Fame, me? Got the intelligence of a flea, who's gonna make me famous? Money? Got all I need. Women? You can keep them, nothing but trouble, they be."

"A wise person. I would pick a wise person for today's Good Deed, wouldn't I?"

We were walking again by then, step by step nearer some little town that I had never seen before and would never see again once I passed through, following the road to wherever it led me.

"Well, I suggest you move on and give someone else a Good Deed for the day, sir. I am content with my walking, thank you. Oh, and thank you for your company for this while, too."

His eyebrows went up. "You mean it, don't you? More and more surprising. I cannot go without leaving you a gift, my friend. One that has no strings attached whatsoever. I will make you a telepath. Then you can use the power of your mind to get what you need when you need it, be it food, clothes or shelter."

It sounded good to me, so I said thanks and he – disappeared. I walked on, content.

And then my problems began.

It was a double edged gift indeed. Oh yes, I could use my power to get what I wanted all right, I had food, clothes, shelter aplenty.

I also knew just what those people thought of me. I had their thoughts coming at me, theirs and everyone else's too. It was as if every person was speaking aloud all the time and I could hear everything.

"Here comes a tramp, hide everything afore he steals it."

"Damn cadgers coming in here, wanting sommat for nothing."

"Suppose we'd better give him a job, send him on his way, he can have that meat, it's been off a couple of days but who cares, he'll be long gone by then."

And the other thoughts:

"I hate him, I wish him dead, I hate him and I want him dead..."

"Could throw her down and do it, couldn't I? What could she say, big man like me..."

"Not enough money to buy food, what am I going to do..."

Every thought, every mood, every variation on every human misery there is.

It battered me, it haunted me; it revolted me. You would not believe what thoughts people hide behind smiling faces. Or perhaps you would, if you've been around long enough to know the true heart of man.

I couldn't stand it.

I went back to where I met him, called to him to take his gift back, begged on my knees for my peaceful existence once more – and then I realised what I had done.

I had scorned a gift from the Devil. He had got his own back in such a subtle way that no one could accuse him of being vindictive.

I also realised it wasn't going to go away.

So I braved the town, as it were, got myself some money, bought myself a load of supplies I thought I would need and some I didn't but have sure come in handy and I left the road, climbed up the mountainside and occupied a cave where I live now. The only thoughts I get up there are birds and animals and they don't bother me none.

I venture down occasionally, brave the battering of the townsfolk, buy more supplies, get my beard and my hair cut and get back up out of the way. And there I'll stay until God or the Devil calls me home.

Well now, I better be off. You're thinking you ain't heard such a load of baloney in a long time, right? I see by your face you were disbelieving and now you have to believe 'cos I nailed it, didn't I, everything you were thinking about me.

I'm going back up there, to my cave, where the thoughts are pure and the air is clean and I stay off them roads.

Guess you could call it road rage, of a kind.

It ain't but with the Devil you don't win. There's them as would have took and took and me, who wanted nothing, got something anyway.

D'you know, thinking on it, I didn't get too bad a deal, did I? I don't walk them endless black strips anymore and I don't have much to do with them there townsfolk and don't that just do me fine?

Just don't let him know where I am, in case he comes a-looking for me with another gift. If that happened, you might find out what road rage is really like.

Cos he won't let me off so easy next time.

Highway Chills

Olivia Arieti

Harold cast a quick glance at his partner, Nick, who had fallen asleep. They had been on the road for more than two days, taking turns at driving. The journeys were all alike, infinite miles ahead, download of the goods and back home; the highways, monotonous, unnerving, with few roadside cafés and not enough parking areas. The more they travelled, the more the destination seemed further, but that was part of the job.

Fortunately it was early fall and the summer haze had given way to the chilly autumn mist.

The driver had known Nick since childhood but never liked him. If their fathers hadn't been lifelong friends, he wouldn't have helped him out. The guy hated working, but loved gambling and by now owed him a lot of money. It had been a mistake taking him in the company. The fact that after such a short time there, he made enough to rent a nice cottage and buy a sports car caused suspicions: sooner or later, he would find out, but at the moment, more important issues were on his mind.

Harold was about to get married; he had finally proposed to Margot, his lover. It had taken him a while to make up his mind for she was a hooker and his rigid mother wouldn't have ever approved. Now that the old lady was dead, he had no restraints.

Whether bewitched or in love, no nights equalled the ones with her; the woman's sensuality was ravishing, her passion unquenchable.

She was totally different from Beatrix, his first fiancée; with sky blue eyes and the sweetest smile, the girl was already an angel while alive. Unfortunately, Beatrix died just a few days before their wedding. The tears and despair that followed were endless, overwhelming. That's when he swore he'd never have a serious affair again and began visiting the hooker. Unpredictably, things took another turn and as time passed, he got more and more attached to her.

After telling Nick his plans, he asked for the money; the spectacular wedding he had in mind was rather expensive, not to mention the honeymoon on the exotic island.

The guy was vexed by his request. He had always envied his friend, the 'good boy', devoted son and hard worker, totally, the opposite of him, a truly depraved and wicked soul. When he was offered the job, he accepted, besides being penniless, he also regarded it as a good opportunity to smuggle what couldn't be legally conveyed.

"Where are we?" asked Nick, yawning and stretching at the same time.

"It's your turn, buddy, want to get a few hours of sleep too."

The sight of the roadside café was most welcomed. Both needed to refresh and some coffee.

The customers at the table near the entrance turned round. They were elderly men, with white hair, dressed in outdated garments. With them was a girl, very pretty even if the face was exaggeratedly pale as if whitened with talcum powder.

"Come and drink your coffee with us, boys, we're always pleased to see new faces around here."

The two drivers looked at each other... How long had these guys been there?

The girl cast an inviting glance at Harold, who sat beside her.

"You must be worn out, nothing more tiring than driving long hours on roads like this," said the oldest looking fellow, his face so decrepit and creased as to appear disfigured.

"Yeah, wait till you reach those hellish turns right before the bridge, got to be wide awake to drive up there," remarked another with a ghastly grin.

"We'll be careful," assured Harold them, he who couldn't remember the turns although the highway wasn't new to him.

"Time to set forth," said Nick, already annoyed by the strange company. He drained his drink.

Just before they got up, the girl let her hand touch Harold's. An instant feeling of warmth pervaded him; their eyes met and the girl blushed and hurriedly lowered hers.

Once on the truck, Harold wondered if he really loved Margot. With Beatrix, his heart throbbed every time he saw her and whenever they kissed, that same warmth entered his whole body... He smiled nostalgically, the casual sensation had been enough to recall such dear memories... His eyes filled with tears, if only she were his bride...

'All that silly lass's fault,' he thought, irate for being so foolishly sentimental, 'and her stupid coquetting.'

To get his mind off such reminiscences, he went over the nuptial arrangements and once again the pressure of the expenses urged him to remind Nick of his debt.

"So you want the bitch to have a glamorous wedding, huh?"

"Don't you dare to call Margot that, you'll regret it."

"Come on, you really can't believe you'll be her only man from now on."

"Your business is to give me back my money, bastard, nothing else."

"Seems you want something more, man."

"Can't wait," declared Harold.

The first parking area was their fighting ring. Both jumped down, their fists already fuelled by wrath.

"And if you really want to know, I've been in her bed long before you and can confirm she's really good at driving a guy wild," Nick sneered just before a punch broke his lip.

"You're rotten, should have never taken you in with me."

"Too bad, you should have known better."

That said, he threw his fist to his face so hard Harold staggered and fell down.

"In hell, that's where you belong!"

"That's where you'll go," his rival shouted just before his last and fatal blow.

"Good, now your bloody money and your gorgeous slag will be mine," he cried.

As a matter of fact, he too had fallen for the hooker, but not only for her... Only when he found out about Harold's affair, he grew terribly jealous and swore he would get her back.

The huge debt and the imminent marriage were too much for him; a strong hatred had seized him and he was glad he had finally freed himself of the 'good boy's' presence.

Now he had to get rid of the body... Thank goodness his partner didn't weigh much. No one was in sight; he managed to drag it to the truck and loaded it just like a bale of merchandise. Afterwards, he would dump it somewhere. The river was not too far ahead...

While driving, he thought of the most appropriate words to break the news to Margot. Who knows? Perhaps, she didn't care at all and after shedding a few due tears, would make love to him that same night; her generous curves and lascivious ways were already kindling his senses. He might even marry her someday, no reason he should share her with other men now that he also had the huge amount stolen from the company's accounts and the one *earned* smuggling....

A good story about poor Harold's death was what he needed and then everything would be over...

He gazed at the road unwinding ahead, satisfied, and kept repeating to himself, 'Well done, man, well done, indeed!'.

Nick's triumphant sensation, however, didn't last long for he began feeling uneasy, worried; although many were the mischiefs he had carried out, that was his first crime.

His mind went back to Harold's bleeding face and agonizing glance. Besides, the mist had grown thicker and the landscape appeared populated by uncanny shadows that sometimes seemed to run alongside the truck as in an eerie race.

The sight of another parking area was a relief. He turned off the engine and took a deep breath; losing control of himself wasn't allowed.

The loud tapping at the window made him shiver; the cadaverous face and clammy hand belonged to the girl they met at the café.

"I'm so happy you're here, Sir, my friends over there are quite in trouble, their van has just broken down."

"I'm no mechanic, but I'll see what I can do, Miss."

On reaching the others, he noticed that they had put up a tent not too far from the van; its whiteness was almost blurring despite the mist. A camp fire had been lit and the flames waved sinisterly against the blackness of the night.

"Thanks for stopping, young man," said one of the guys, the voice raucous, the glance piercing his soul. "It's good seeing you again.".

"I'm a bit in a hurry, but I'll have a look," he replied hastily, fearful they might ask about his partner.

"First come in here with us, I'm sure you need a strong cup of coffee, it shows on your face," and the familiar ghastly grin followed.

Could something else show on his face?

"Do come in," exhorted one of the others and placed his bony hand on his arm.

The inside was cold and damp as though the tent had been up for ages. The light of two lanterns shed a red glow on the men's faces and Nick felt uncomfortable.

"Say, that's quite a big truck out there, what are you carrying?" asked one in an inquisitive tone.

"Several types of goods."

"I bet they're perishable," sneered another.

All remained silent, then stared at Nick as though waiting for a confession.

"We, too, have a job, man, got to report what happens on this damned highway to our boss," said a guy who had just entered the tent, up to then a stranger to the driver, "and we believe we should have a look of what's inside your truck."

He was so skeletal and emaciated that Nick wondered how he could stand on his feet.

Could they have seen what happened while passing by?

The fact is that our little girl here is impatient… still has some feelings for the poor chap."

A sweet smile brightened her face. "It wasn't exactly how I expected, but it's such a joy to have him back." And added, "Just in time."

Nick was startled. What were those mad folks talking about? Who were they?

The same bony hand grasped his arm, "Bring him out, no chance of getting away with it."

Chills ran down his spine; they knew about the murder.

'Better beat it,' he thought, leaping up and running out, ready to jump on the truck and disappear, but the odd fellows were already in front of the vehicle.

"Can't wait any longer, man, it's almost dawn and *we*'re the ones in a hurry."

A spellbound Nick did as told.

Harold's body was lying placidly as if in a deep slumber.

"Now bury him," said a guy whose dark robe recalled the reaper man's one. He handed him a spade. "A dignified burial is what every soul deserves."

"Wait," cried the girl, "let me kiss him... We've been separated so violently," and gently put her lips on his.

Nick shuddered on seeing his victim's eyes roll slightly and look at her.

After burying the corpse, he stood waiting for what might happen next, but all the bystanders turned their backs to him and entered the tent.

Much to his surprise, nobody seemed opposed to his departure.

He cast a glance at the creepy shelter; the fire had died and the mist that by then had turned into a plumbeous fog, let visible only an ominous mass that quickly disappeared.

No sooner he was on the road again than also the weirdoes' features faded...

Surely, nothing but horrible hallucinations due to his excessive agitation. The crime had driven him mad and perhaps, that was his punishment.

Whatever, the body was no longer on the truck and therefore, there was no reason to be afraid.

He was doing his best to calm down, when a sequence of sharp turns appeared before him, the road narrowed and suddenly the speed increased; the vehicle was totally out of control.

On the bridge, it hit the railing and fell straight into the murky waters.

Harold and Beatrix's shadows, hand in hand, stood watching the final scene.

73

Cosmic Spin Class on Deck 112

SJ Townend

Varde was waiting to be scanned in to the Health & Leisure deck. She pulls on her blue unitard sleeves. Beneath it, her skin feels too small, but the instructions state the attire is obligatory.

"Eleventh door on the left," the receptionist says. Varde's eyes are questing in the other direction, searching for another glimpse of the happy family: a couple sandwiching a child, swinging the young boy with dimples like Benjamin had, five, maybe six Earth years old, in between them. It's no use, she gives up; they're lost to the crowds of holidaymakers and off duty star-sailors. She now only hears the reverberation of his laughter, feels its tight squeeze on her heart. "Your treatment commences in three minutes."

"Sure," Varde replies, her voice reedy, unsure. "Thanks."

The eleventh door opens automatically on her approach. Hydraulic magnets hiss, the noise dissipates, becomes lost between the whir and flick of wheels. Inside the padded box room are seven others in blue skinsuits, all taking in the blurred bucolic projections on the walls and ceiling, all already in their spots, cycling, disinterested in her arrival, self-absorbed.

The therapist-cum-instructor, green unitard, greets Varde, "Welcome to the wellbeing trial." He guides her to the last vacant fixed-position bicycle, lowers the seat, helps her ascend. "Comfortable?" he asks. She notices: the man smacks of vitality, there is no depression in his eyes; his pupils—ambertone, sparkling—are not the shade of ghosts others tell her hers have become. *He has not seen death,* she thinks. She nods and forces a tight-lipped, defiant smile, *this therapy will not help me.* The instructor returns to the front, mounts his counterposed bike.

She starts to pedal, it does not come naturally—it has been so long since her calf muscles, her lungs, have felt the burn of exercise. *This will hurt tomorrow,* she thinks, *but it'll be no match for the abyss spreading in my soul.*

***

Varde was issued with a formal ultimatum by her line manager—take the experimental therapy, or return to Earth—she had almost laughed at the irony. *Return* to Earth? She'd never *been* to Earth. She had been born aboard the ship, as had Benjamin, her son, she knew little about the blue-green ball of pollution and had no intention of finding out anything further. Intergalactic Cruiser-3024X was her home. She'd remain on board until Death said otherwise. Her own ashes would be ejected and scattered in space, to become stardust once more, for this was the done thing for a star-sailor, not to be buried under six foot of gravity-shackled, alien soil.

***

Nine corrugated tubes concertina down from the ceiling. At the end of each, a mask. She yanks down the one above her station, she follows the direction of the instructor, places it over her mouth and nose, pulls the strap behind her head tight with one hand and maintains her balance with the other. The instructor flicks a switch on his visual display unit. *Phhhssshhhh.* A funky brown gas discharges, steams down the tubing.

"In.. out," the instructor chants, his demonstration mask retracting up towards the ceiling, "breathe in time with your footwork."

Top notes of portabello carbonara, fusty mildew, something similar to the archaic ale served to old timers down on the retirement deck permeate her olfactory system. Potent aromatic medicinal vapours penetrate her blood-tissue barrier, adulterates each organ, messes with her intracellular receptors. Her pineal gland welcomes the novel spores. More scented research pharmaceuticals extracted from wounded Tentilus suppurations gush into the confinement of her plastic mask. Her bronchi are flooded, her alveoli drenched.

"Faster," the instructor commands. Her legs birl in time with his vocal outbursts. *This alien pus vapour is repulsive, thank heck this stage is transient,* she reminds hersel, and pedals through the insufflations, knowing the mask should deliver oxygen soon.

She closes her eyes, focuses only on breath-work, the push and the pull of the pedals. She feels the accumulation of lactic acid in her thighs, prays for the elusive endorphins to arrive, the healing to begin.

"One two, one two," the instructor counts, his voice the only offering of music or rhythm. The last words she hears are 'astral projection' and the instructor's voice is replaced with the *thud thud thud* of her heart, the whoosh of blood through her ears. She opens her eyes: the instructor, gone, the other guinea pigs, gone.

One cyclist remains, but it's not who was there before. The feet of this cyclist dangle far from the pedals. Naked bar underwear—the pants with the oafish teddy bears on—their countenance is wan, nondescript. The boy's feverish, dewy skin is riddled with deathly Jupiter Pox, each papule blackening, a widening black hole.

"Benjamin?" she wants to say, her mouth, useless.

"Pedal faster, Mother." The apparition speaks. Her heart swells, feels like it may burst, open up its red, but it does not. She keeps pedalling, unsure if she's trying to escape or move closer to this diaphanous silhouette of her dead son. The boy, now more pox, more encroaching black void than skin, is vanishing, about to leave her for a second time. Before she has a chance to summon a whisper of his name, he becomes devoured by the expanse of galaxial, swirling pustules. Gone.

The periphery of her vision—rolling bucolic videodrome—retreats, becomes replaced by darkness as the drug kicks in and she becomes lost in the depths of a cerebral thalassic journey. She is no longer clad in Lycra, perched on a bike, she now swims: weightless, lightless, afraid, hopeful.

She is liberated, she twirls round. Her body moves, oil in water. As she turns, her eyes narrow, her body arches forward, cups back. She draws in sharp a lungful of void. Is she *outside* the spaceship now?

In front of her, shining like a celestial candelabra, she witnesses it: All Of The Light. Flickering ruby, garnet and amethyst jewels dimple the incandescent, golden nebula. Colours blare out their majestic orchestral synaesthesia for her eyes only. And her eyes, still squinting, adjust and with her hands, she paddles backwards through water which is now not water, but the lacuna of deep space, and she looks again, tries to gain a better perspective. Breathing freely, the fungal stench of the drug trial no more, she now inhales sweet star anise, ozone, asteroid gunmetal, talc and the reminiscent scent of newborn.

And she knows this is not the Eagle Nebulae with its pillars of creation, this is something else, something better, something long forgotten. It encompasses her field of vision. Unclear, diffuse edges form a gentle shape. Undulating ripples of grey-white-orange love frill out, caress and overwhelm her. The colossal interstellar gas cloud rests in the form of a smiling child, a child reclined on its side. Benjamin.

A crack of curved light spreads where his lips would be, a smile. His skinscape is mottled, not with pox this time, this place, but with gigantic, cosmic pools, each constantly in slow labour, forever birthing new stars, new worlds.

The Child Nebula winks at her, a hundred new galaxies spin free from its eye socket, fling into space like exploding plant pods dispersing seeds in high pressure bursts. Varde hears his laughter— *Benjamin*—and then, she is back in the box room, seven blue cyclists and one green instructor surround her. She stops pedalling, pulls off the mask.

It is true, she thinks, *stardust. I have seen death and now I have seen re-birth, but I will never hold him in my arms again.*

Here Comes Cowboy Death

Rie Sheridan Rose

Here comes Cowboy Death
with his steel-toed boots –
heels clicking like
coffin nails on concrete.
He grins his cow skull grin
with hat tilted jauntily and
his finger bones jitter
like Spanish castanets.
There's a gleam of madness
in his hollow eyes
and behind their
witch-lights
squirm maggots
spinning his thoughts
like silkworms.
He rides a horse of
jet black bones
with mane of fire
and hooves that spark
the streets they pass.
Do you hear him coming?
The snick of hooves,
The click of boots?
Here comes Cowboy Death…
And he's scouting for souls.

People Eaters

Rickey Rivers Jr.

1.

Don't find yourself alone with people eaters. They aren't zombies. They're people eating people. People who're talking and coherent and alive one moment, then they're right after you, wanting you, ready to eat you. After they've eaten, they're normal again. Like nothing happened at all.

For me the people eating started at home. I was in the kitchen with my wife, Clara, and my daughter, Riley. We we're having a normal breakfast. At some point Clara grabbed onto Riley and took a bite out of her arm. She then grabbed a hand and bit into it.

I sat there a moment, overwhelmed. Riley was screaming her head off. I took action once Clara had wrestled Riley to the kitchen floor and bit off her nose. I snapped out of my shock and pulled Clara off her. I then tended to Riley. She was bleeding out and crying, her lips shook, she couldn't speak. A final gurgle told me the future. Her body was moving and wanting the words. Then she was still. With my dead daughter in my arms I looked over to my wife and she was licking her lips. She looked back at me and frowned. Then she screamed.

"What happened to Riley?"

At this moment I didn't know if madness had taken her. Either that or she was trying to lure me into some sort of trap. Clara screamed once more.

"What happened? What did you do?"

She crawled over to us and cried. Again, I was dumbfounded. All of this happened so fast. It was like a minute had gone by. Clara looked at me with teary eyes and asked me over and over again what happened. She kept saying "Why?" The same word I had in my head. Why was it happening? Why hadn't she remembered?

I took Riley to her room. I didn't know what else to do, it just made sense. I took her bloody, lifeless body and laid her on her bed. She liked her room. It was pretty. Clara and I painted it colors we thought she'd like. Riley just liked a place to herself.

Clara kept in the kitchen, crying on the floor. I kept with Riley. Because the dead person was the only sane person left in the house. That was the case, must have been, because it all didn't make any sense.

***

At some point I broke myself out of a daze and left Riley in her room. I went to the telephone and tried to call the police. I started dialing but hung up. I put a hand to head and cried. Clara heard me crying and came to me. She was still crying, mixing tears with the blood on her chin, the dried blood, Riley's blood.

She hugged me. I told her everything would be alright. I was wrong, but sometimes you say that for

82

the other person. I went to the living room and turned on the news. That's another thing you do when things happen. You see if other people know. You see if they can help you. I was hoping they could. I was hoping the news had instructions for this situation. I needed the news to tell me that this was worldwide or something, anything, that it was affecting more people than Clara.

The news reported that several people had been attacked by others. Bitten and the biter being confused yet coherent, still 'themselves' after all. They'd scream for help after biting someone and run in different directions. It wasn't just Clara and that was good. I didn't want to have to deal with this alone.

After seeing the news, Clara said "That's terrible." And I just looked at her. I couldn't even say anything. If I did I'd strangle her next. She wouldn't know why either. It was a cruel thing, to be angry, to know the perpetrator, to not be able to punish them. I hated inaction. I couldn't do anything.

The news continued coverage about the incidents. A man in Florida was interviewed. He was crying. He said his son and daughter had eaten his wife. He said he sat there watching. He was unable to move. Then his children saw their meal and started crying. They ran to him, hugged him. They asked, "What happened to Mommy?" The man was looking at the news camera with a wide eyed expression, total shock. It was like he speaking to me directly. He was a shell now, shattered, a wide eyed shell of a man. In that instance, we understood each other. His eyes told a terrible story, much louder than words could say. I felt his grief.

***

I slept in Riley's room that night. I didn't want to sleep in the same room with Clara. I let her have our bedroom.

The day after, the President gave a speech. He stopped halfway and tore into the Vice President. Everyone just let the President eat. Then his meal was pulled off stage. The President's mouth was wiped and he went on with his speech. He stated that everything was under control, that they were increasing military efforts in small towns and areas where the attacks had been most prominent. I didn't trust it. Shooting a bunch of people wouldn't help. Everything was normalizing, and much too fast for me.

2.

Clara was screaming at me today. I woke up with a salty tongue and a wet face. I'd been crying. Apparently I also partook in eating a child. That's what she kept saying.

"You were chewing his face."

Don't know what that's about. People have been doing it for a while, attacking and eating others. Clara said we saw a news report about it. I don't remember that. I asked about Riley and Clara said she was dead in her room. I didn't believe her. I tried to turn the car around. Clara swerved me back from turning and referred to the blood on my shirt and the blood on hers. I asked what happened. She said she didn't know. I don't know what's going on, but we're on the road and far from home. How long was out?

***

The radio works. A man on a talk radio show gave out the location to a safe haven. I guess we're going there. Clara keeps looking at me with wide eyes. What's wrong with her?

After some time she tells me we're headed to get food, then to the safe haven.

"Protection," she says, "protection."

The man on the radio says something about people eaters. It doesn't make sense. I just want to go home and bury our daughter.

"Protection," says Clara, "protection."

I nod. What else can I do?

Clara says there's safety in numbers and I agree. People should be around other people. Even when something unexplained is going on. We should still be around each other, to protect each other. Isolation is suicide. Clara agreed.

With other people we can look out for each other. And we're taking food too. That's good. The safe haven must have food as well. That's good too. That's the plan. It's a sound plan, everyone brings their own food. We'll be safe. The food will be in one place, all the food in one place.

I Am the Night Prowler

David Turnbull

I woke one morning with a metallic tang in my mouth and an odd humming in my chest. My arms and legs felt stiff. I shuffled awkwardly to the bathroom and splashed cold water on my face. My hands smelled of rubber. In the mirror my eyes gleamed like headlights. The cups of my ears seemed to glint in the morning sunlight, as if they themselves housed mirrors. I coughed and a low growl emitted from my throat.

Was I ill? About to have a seizure or stroke? Or was I still so deep in the thralls of grief that I was suffering some sort of hallucination triggered by my mental anguish? I got dressed, fetched my car keys and made my devoted daily drive to the shrine. The roadside memorial I had created for my wife and six year-old daughter, killed in a road traffic accident at the intersection four months earlier.

It was a simple tribute. Monica's favourite silk scarf wrapped around the neck of Kira's favourite teddy-bear, which was, in turn, attached by plastic ties to the lamppost nearest to where they'd been killed. Above the teddy-bear a photo in a frame was similarly tied to the lamppost. The photo had been taken by me, Monica and Kira smiling for the camera on the beach in Benidorm, each holding a whipped ice cream cone, swirled with raspberry sauce.

I felt increasingly stiff so I parked my car and stepped out. In the days after the accident, friends and relatives had set out floral tributes at the foot of the lamppost. These were withered now, almost gone to dust. The teddy-bear and scarf were rain sodden and caked with roadside grime. The glass in the picture frame had steamed up through condensation.

I cried. I always did when I visited. The progress of tears down my cheek felt strangely slow and sluggish. When I reached up to wipe them away the residue on my fingers had the constituency and translucency of engine oil.

I wondered if it was time to attempt go back to work. I'd been employed by my firm for almost a decade. Longer than Kira had been alive. They were showing a lot of compassion. The MD had said I should take as much time as I needed to grieve. But sixteen weeks was a long, long time. I should really get myself back into the swing of engaging with people. My self-imposed isolation was clearly causing me mental health issues.

`A sudden jarring pain up the left side of my leg suggested this might now be having some sort of knock-on psychosomatic impact. I stood beside my little shrine for a while longer, as I always did, telling my wife and daughter how much I loved them. How my heart ached till it hurt from the soul-destroying sense of loss I felt. When my hands began to stiffen, I decided the safest thing for me to do would be to drive back home.

***

I hadn't had much of an appetite since the funeral. I was looking gaunt, having shed a few pounds. But when I arrived home, I felt famished. Not just famished, absolutely ravenous. There was nothing but a carton of milk in the fridge, on the cusp of turning sour. I raided the cupboards for canned food. Soup and baked beans and corned beef and sardines. I wolfed them down, not even bothering to remove them from their tins.

Judders jolted through me, sparking like sparkplugs, sending blood gushing through the tubes of my veins and arteries. The metallic tang in my mouth intensified. My teeth felt odd. Like hard plastic, set in the dashboard of my gums. I opened my hands and looked at the palms. There were deep, dark treads where the lines should be.

I ate some more. A jar of black olives. A can of chopped tomatoes. Some Spam.

The stiffness in my body seemed to solidify.

I lay down on the sofa and was aware I had begun to snore, growling like an engine ticking over.

I dreamed I was him. The pampered brat who had taken my family from me. The kid, barely out of secondary school, who had snatched them from existence as easily as a magician snapping his fingers.

I dreamed I was behind the wheel of the gun metal grey, four-wheel drive Kia Sorrento his indulgent parents had bought for his eighteenth birthday. A vehicle far too powerful for someone who had only passed his driving test on his third attempt less than a month earlier. A vehicle, transformed by those circumstances, into a murderous weapon.

I dreamed I was showing off to my girlfriend who was in the passenger seat and my two friends in the back. Top of the range hifi system pounding out the kind of beats we'd been clubbing to all night. All of us still high on the coke we'd been snorting and mojitos we'd been necking.

I was laughing and joking, throwing banter back and forth with my friends. The early morning October sun was low in the sky, causing a glare that limited my vision. But I wasn't paying attention anyway. I was going too fast, gunning the foot peddle. I didn't see the woman on the crossing, holding hands with her daughter, on their way to a doctor's appointment before school.

I didn't see them till I hit them and they tumbled skywards. Then I was screaming and slamming my foot on the brake far too late. I heard the wheels skidding as the Kia slammed into a wall and glass showered my head and face.

And then I was out on the street, bleeding from numerous lesions. And my girlfriend was doubled over by the concertina wreck of the Kia, endlessly vomiting. And one of my friends was clutching his broken arm. My other friend was staggering along the pavement, dazed and concussed. I was yelling that one of them had to say that they were driving, not me. And half a dozen pedestrians running to the aid of the woman and her daughter witnessed this selfish outburst and later relayed that in statements to the police.

Then I saw the little girl, like a rag doll strewn on the road, neck twisted, blood pooling around her head. And I compounded my childish callousness by trying to shift the blame. Yelling at the tiny pale corpse. "Why were you in the middle of the road? Were you not watching where you were going?"

That was when I sucked breath as my eyes snapped open, waking me up at the point in the dream where I always woke. As usual my mind went back over the apology the police family liaison officer kept offering for the length of time it was taking to bring the matter to trial. I heard the warning she frequently gave me that if the case wasn't brought before a judge within six months the driver couldn't be tried. And I found myself consumed again by the paranoid suspicion that somehow the boy's wealthy parents were bringing undue influence to bear to deliberately slow the process down.

It was dusk outside, pink disc of the February sun setting in a pink hued sky. I drank another can of soup, glugging it down straight from the open tin. Then I devoured an entire pack of digestive biscuits. My hunger seemed insatiable. I was like a marathon runner storing fuel for the big event.

My arms and legs felt so stiff they were almost rigid. My spine felt as if it had a steel chassis running through it. When I looked in the mirror my eyes gleamed and my ears glinted. When I lifted my shirt, I saw my ribs had begun to protrude like a radiator grill.

It occurred to me that going for a little jog around the block might help loosen me up and shake me out of whatever post trauma event was making me imagine all of this was real. I pulled on an old tracksuit, but when I tried to slip into my trainers I found they wouldn't fit my severely swollen feet. The hard, rubbery texture had afflicted the soles of my feet so I figured it would be fine to risk running barefoot. If I stepped on a sharp stone or a nail the pain might snap me back to a semblance of reality.

My gait was awkward, gambolling and lurching along on legs that seemed only capable of bending a fraction at the knee. The moon was rising, fat and full and yellow. The stars were sprouting like glitter on a black sheet of silk. All of this seemed to hasten what I still perceived to be a sort of grief driven delusion.

The pain of it felt real, however. Bones hardening, joints stiffening. The moon grew fatter and it began to rain, its glow becoming shrouded in a silvery haze. I staggered and stumbled, grazing my knee when I fell. The blood that trickled from the broken flesh was black and syrupy, viscous as oil.

The rain began to fall heavier, rebounding from the pavement, rushing along the gutters, slices of it illuminated by the headlights of cars passing by. I didn't think that in my condition I would be able to get home. I staggered into the car park of a leisure centre long closed for redevelopment, hoping to shelter in its boarded doorway till the rain stopped and the strange malaise which had seized me had abated.

I was about half way across the carpark when my body began to fit and spasm. I dropped to my knees in one of the potholed parking bays. More black blood gushed from my wound. My head snapped painfully back against my spine. My hands bunched to tight fists and began to roll inward, gathering my arms as they went. My feet and legs did likewise.

My innards and organs displaced and relocated. I screamed in utter anguish and agony. My hips broadened to impossible geometric angles. My torso grew gigantically in both length and breadth. Shredded rags of my tracksuit were blown from me by the gusting wind.

I found myself on four evenly spaced wheels, rain lashing on metallic flesh, imbued with multi-directional smoked glass vision.

My disfigurement settled to its new distorted form. I felt my heart roar with combustion as oil pumped through my coiled veins. I rolled forward and felt the crunch of grit beneath the rolled-up rubber of my limbs. I saw streetlights and buildings rising around me. I saw the entrance to the car park and the black road that passed by like a wide tarmac river. Wipers streaked rain from my windscreen like eyelids blinking away tears.

My mechanical heart revved and smoky exhalations of breath gushed from my oesophagus exhaust pipe. I rolled out onto the road and felt the wet tar beneath my wheels. I trundled cautiously along, not fathoming how I was gathering my momentum, uncertain as to whether I was dreaming, hallucinating or experiencing an actual physical phenomenon.

I came to a red light and idled there. I saw my reflection in a shop window. I had taken the form of a saloon car, smoked windows, paintwork of such a dark shade of green it was almost black. Beneath the beat of the rain I looked sleek and malevolent and predatory. But, somehow, I also looked inexplicably like myself. I was unmistakably me. As if all of my molecules had been tossed skyward and reformed in an entirely different structure which managed against the odds to retain the essence of who I was and what I was and all I should be.

The lights turned green. I moved forward, experimentally picking up speed, throwing up spray like a child splashing in puddles, experiencing a joyful elation as I took corners. Blink-blink-blink went the streetlights as I passed from one to the next. Ratatatat went the rain against my bonnet and my rooftop.

***

When I approached the intersection, from my newfound perspective it seemed to look like a crucifix. The main road I was traversing was the body of the cross, the smaller roads to the left and right its arms. And at its centre point my shrine to Monica and Kira, with its teddy bear and scarf and photo of them beneath the clouded glass of the frame.

They were there, my wife and daughter, standing forlorn amongst the disintegrating remnants of the floral tributes. It seemed my altered physical form had tuned my perception to the sweet spot where I could see into the land of the dead. I didn't like what I saw. It pained and aggrieved me.

They stood in the same pose as they had in the picture I'd taken in Benidorm, Monica slightly behind Kira, both of them holding smudgy facsimiles of ice cream cones. Blood, rather than raspberry sauce, oozing over the whipped peaks of the ice cream. The blood they'd shed on the road when they were tossed skyward to crash fatally down. But it was their faces that drew me and filled me with dread. Pale and elongated, slightly distorted, eyes and mouths wide, in perfect circles, like the distraught character in the famous painting by Edward Munch.

I could hear the confusion and desolation in the single word they were screaming repetitively over and over. *Why? Why? Why? Why?* I felt so helpless. They were in distress. But I couldn't think of a single thing I might do to help them.

My engine revved. I sped away. No thought as to where I was heading.

I found myself on the dual carriageway which circumnavigates the town. Traffic was reasonably light, tail end of rush hour. I felt as if I was part of a migration of sleek primordial creatures. I picked up speed, overtaking and weaving between lanes. Drivers honked their horns and flashed their lights.

I paid them no heed. I was different to the vehicles they drove. I was an upgrade, the alpha male, the stallion of the herd. Accountable only to the moon. My horn blared like a whoop. Loud music roared from my speakers. A cavalcade of the songs Monica and I loved to listen to. The playlist of my subconscious mind.

When I almost ran into the back of a slow moving delivery truck I realised how reckless I was being. This was how accidents happened. This was how people got killed. Surely I hadn't undergone this transformation in order to commit a crime as heinous as the one which had robbed me of my wife and daughter?

I took the next exit and slowed down as I passed along the quiet roads of leafy suburbia. The houses were big here. Lush green lawns behind tall privet bushes and electronic security gates. I drove ever more slowly. The volume of my mind music fell low. I passed a white house with tall windows and an ornate veranda. The sign above the electronic card reader at the front gate read *Casa Gonsalla*.

A few yards along the road I came to a halt. Gonsalla. That was his name. The teenage driver of the murderous Kia. Anthony Gonsalla, son of a restaurateur who owned six Italian restaurants and a pizza delivery chain.

I found myself reversing back to the gate. I could see a long gravel driveway, bounded on either side, shrubs trimmed in topiary into depictions of various animals. Two cars sat to the front of the house, a vintage Bentley and a Range Rover. A few months back the Kia would have sat there too. Days slowly ticking towards that fatal instant at the intersection.

I reversed a little more and came to a halt in a little dark spot in the gap between two streetlights shrouded by a tall pine. My engine stopped. My headlights blinked out. The music faded away. I sat in silence. The rain began to ease. Ahead of me the moon was hazily reflected in the surface water gathered on road.

I wondered if Mr and Mrs Gonsalla were home. Preparing for bed, oblivious to my strange presence outside their house. I wondered if they felt any guilt for what their son had done. He was their only child. They'd spoiled him to the point that his immediate reaction to his wrongdoing was to take it for granted that someone else would accept the blame. In my eyes they were as culpable as their son. They had started a chain of events that ended in death and the destruction of a happy family.

n the silence beneath the moon, the rain becoming a fine, misty drizzle, I pondered the impossible thing I had become. Had some supernatural phenomenon truly transformed me to metal and rubber? Engine for a heart and oil for blood? Or was I experiencing a deep psychosis? Had I ran pell-mell through the streets, rather than driven through them? Was I standing beneath the pine, rather than parked at the kerb?

Was I the sleek saloon car I'd seen in the reflection in the window?

Was I still the fragile, grieving human I had been for months?

Was I some strange hybrid of both?

A set of headlights approaching from the other end of the street snapped me out of my thoughts.

The car slowed and came to a halt at the other side of the gates. A little illuminated sign on its roof read *TAXI*. The passenger door to the rear swung open and someone staggered drunkenly onto the pavement. The driver rolled down his window. The drunk leaned in and handed over his fare. The taxi pulled away and swerved as it passed me.

The drunk approached the gates. It was him. Anthony Gonsalla. The man-child responsible for the deaths of my wife and daughter. The reason their ghosts stood by their shrine, endlessly repeating that unanswered question – *Why? Why? Why?*

He was wearing expensive designer clothing and, somewhat ridiculously, wearing sunglasses despite it being the middle of the night. Clearly his parents had seen sense and not let him loose on another vehicle. But equally clearly his recklessness had not put paid to his habits. He was inebriated and high as kite. As he had been on that day.

I felt the anger boil within me as he staggered and fumbled, attempting to punch in the entry code for the gates. My thoughts raced. *I could get my revenge in that instant, rev my engine, speed forward, toss him into the air, see the crack of his skull in my rear-view mirror, and reverse over his dying body for good measure. Or I could ram him against the gates. Leave him crippled, condemned for the rest of his life by being confined to a wheelchair.*

My engine growled. My headlights went on. Anthony turned and removed his sunglasses, holding his hand over his eyes to protect them from the glare. My wheels rolled forward. Just as I was about to pick up speed, the gates swung inward. By the time I reached them they were closing. Anthony's father dressed in pyjamas and a dressing gown stood there with his delinquent son on their driveway and watched me prowl slowly past.

***

I found myself back in the car park in human form, naked, shivering. The morning sun stung my eyes. Through narrow eyelids I saw shredded remnants of the tracksuit blowing around the potholes. I was ravenous. My stomach so hollow it ached with a pain that momentarily doubled me over.

I winced from the knot in my belly then found an overloaded skip. I found a set of workman's white dungarees, splattered in yellow paint and crusted with dried plaster. I managed to pull them on. They were still damp from the night rain. My teeth chattered as I walked bare footed back home.

The first thing I did when I reached home was to devour everything I could find left in the cupboards but still the hunger gnawed at me. I took a shower, dressed in some fresh clothes, threw the builder's dungarees in the bin, grabbed my keys and set off to drive to the supermarket.

The roads were a revelation. My recent experience had caused me to view cars and trucks and buses as organic lifeforms. They were like the mighty lions and other beasts of the Serengeti. Wild and unpredictable. If you stepped into their territory at the wrong moment, the consequences could be dire.

There was a new shrine at the roundabout. A bicycle spray painted white, a picture of a boy of around twelve or thirteen, dozens of floral tributes. I discovered through an article in the free newspaper I picked up that his name was Mohan Khan. He'd been knocked from his bike and run over while on his way home from football practice at secondary school. The driver of the car that hit him was found to be twice the legal limit when the traffic police breathalysed him.

Another reckless driver.

Another needless death.

Another grieving father.

***

The moon was full again and I took to the roads, once more transformed into the saloon car. It seemed that my shapeshifting was triggered by lunar cycles. Perhaps there is truth in the old lycanthrope legends? Perhaps the transformation matches the age in which you live? After all, these days a car is far more likely to end your life than a wolf.

It felt so good to feel the touch of rubber against tarmac. To feel the whoosh of air as I sped along. To see the yellow glint of the moon reflected in my gleaming green bonnet. To be once more in the domain of the metal beasts, engine growling, carbon monoxide gushing from my exhaust.

I parked by the shrine. My wife and daughter stood there, bloody ice-creams in their hands, faces distorted and contorted, repeating over and over and over – *Why? Why? Why? Why?*

My back door swung open, as if I was holding out an arm to embrace them. They came gliding eerily forward and settled themselves side by side in the back seat. My door clicked shut. I played them a song. One of our favourites, one that we'd played many times on family car journeys.

I thought I might feel some sort of elation at having them so intimately close to me. Instead, I felt chilled to the core and filled with a melancholy sadness. This was not them. This was a fragment of time, captured and cursed to repeat like a needle stuck on a record. This was the moment they saw the Kia, the second before it hit them. *Why? Why? Why?* these poor, ensnared entities intoned, as the blood dripped from their whipped cones to my upholstery.

My engine purred. The purr became a growl. I pulled away from the kerb and left the shrine behind. I passed through the streets, watching my reflection in shop windows, seeing my number plate, MK 1610, my ghostly passengers sitting side by side, repeating their mantra – *Why? Why? Why?*

Onto the dual carriageway, measuring my speed, equally respectful of the elephantine lumbering trucks as I was of the dart and weave of the gazelle like motorbikes that changed from lane to lane. Songs we loved following one after the other. Then down the slip road to the suburbs and to *Casa Gonsalla.*

I parked myself once more beneath the tall pine, in that shadowy place between the streetlights. My engine stopped. My headlights blinked out. The music faded. I imagined I was talking and found voice emerging in static whispers from the stereo speakers. I reminisced about things we'd done and places we'd been. I speculated on what Kira might have become had she been given the chance to live and how proud Monica and myself would have been of her.

I got nothing in return.

Just that endless unanswered question.

Why? Why? Why?

It may have been two hours or more before I saw the headlights approach from the other end of the street. Anthony Gonsalla had habits and addictions, but he was also a creature of habit. Wherever he went at night to squander his parents' hard-earned cash he always came home to the sanctity of the family home.

I watched him emerge from the taxi and lean in toward the driver's window in a virtual replay of the events I had witnessed on the previous occasion. I watched the taxi pull away. I watched him stagger to the gate. In the back seat Monica and Kira, seeming to sense his presence, grew more and more agitated.

Why? Why? Why?

My door swung open. They got out, bloodied ice creams held out before them as they juddered along the pavement, beseeching their killer to answer their question. *Why? Why? Why?*

101

Anthony was bent over, fumbling with the keypad. His head cocked to one side as if he was hearing them. When he looked round and saw their dreadful approach, he let out a cry of alarm. I could tell from the look of abject terror etched on his face that he recognised them. He knew exactly who they were. He shook as head as if trying to convince himself that what he was seeing was some sort of narcotic induced nightmare vision.

The shock of it gave him sufficient sobriety to accurately punch in the key code. He dashed through before the gates were fully open. Monica and Kira followed him, gory ice creams in their spectral hands, repeating their question. *Why? Why? Why?*

My engine sparked to life and I rolled forward. I saw Anthony fleeing between the topiary toward the front door of the white villa. The relentless remnants of my wife and daughter were so close there was no prospect of him getting into the house without them following.

This was good.

He deserved to be tormented by them for the rest of his days. I paused a moment to watch as this played out. Then I set off, imbued with a sense of relief and achievement.

I had learned from the experience of my previous night prowl and had left a plastic bag of clean clothing and shoes stuffed behind the skip in the carpark. I made my way back through streets largely empty of traffic at that early hour. I took a detour via the roundabout near the supermarket.

And he was there at his shrine, standing beside his white, painted bike. The ghost of Mohan Khan, dressed in his football kit and football boots, pale brown complexion tainted with the grey wan of death, mouth wide, face contorted, the football he held in his hands streaked with the blood he'd shed on the road. Like Monica and Kira he was trapped in that moment before the car hit him, endlessly repeating the question. *Why? Why? Why?*

***

And now here I am, rapidly demolishing the banquette I have set out on my kitchen table, ravenously replenishing my depleted fuel reserves. The events of last night have lifted me. I feel a lightness I have not felt for a long, long time.

When I am sated, I will dismantle my roadside shrine. Sweep away the disintegrating flowers and put the photo and teddy bear into plastic bags for safe keeping. I know now that the shrine was an anchor that held myself and my departed family in that bad place. It had me returning there over and over as if I myself were the revenant. It prevented Monica and Kira from doing what ghosts ought to do.

Now they haunt Anthony Gonsalla, persecuting him with their persistent question.

All is as it should be.

And I have a new sense of purpose.

Four weeks before the lunar cycle swells the moon once more. Four weeks before my next transformation and I feel tar beneath rubber. Four weeks in which to find out all I can about Mohan Khan's killer. Who he is and where he lives. Under the moonlight I will drive the boy's tormented spirit from the shrine his family made to where he truly needs to be, to the person who rightfully deserves tormenting.

There are other shrines across my county, in the towns and along the A roads. I will visit them all. See what I can see. Do what I can do. I have wheels; I can travel further afield if necessary. I am the night prowler. I roam the streets at night. Know me by number plate. MK 1610. Fear me if you have something on your conscience.

Garden Path

SJ Townend

Imagine a dense, cold forest: a liminal place; dim, like the dying glow of a near-spent candle at midnight; crisp and soulless, all derelict church of flora. The forest at the end of the garden path is unlike any you've ever ventured into before and it is believed a magic of sorts lurks within it.

Howsoever, not all magic is good, but not all forests are bad and sometimes it's the creatures who reside underneath or around the branch-rich holt who smack of evil. Sometimes it's those who venture into the forest, always expecting, expecting, expecting, who bring forth the turpitudinous ruckus.

But sometimes it is the trees.

The inhabitants of the hamlet of Monkton knew it was unwise to build within the nearby forest but once, a distant, long-lost relative of a friend of a friend of someone you may or may not know *did* attempt to build a small dwelling within said woods. They abandoned it shortly after completion after an encounter with a Something.

Rumours about what caused the settler to flee ricocheted from one household to the next, retellings travelled like feathers in a breeze of dragon sneeze over the years that followed. Villagers who dared approach the edge of the woods, keen to challenge the claims of what resided within, said they heard the message of warning unfurl in whispers directly from the trees themselves: '*here be not a friendly place*'.

The Something—a witch or a wizard, no-one dared venture close enough to know—became known as The Witchard. What was known about this being you ponder? Well, The Witchard owned a sorrowful face and long white hair full of more knots than a well-trained sailor would ever be able to unfashion and was said to dress in a cloak of dried autumn foliage woven together with iridescent cobwebs. Talk said too it had deep-sunk eyes, black like obsidian.

Despite the fear, the forest suggested, the countryside around it was beautiful and blessed with rich, fertile soils, so a cluster of farms and cottages built up around its thicketed perimeter. But through generations, fervent heed was taken: no further fool attempted to build their home in the woods; no-one set foot where the trees of the forest cast their ominous shade; no-one went in or near the domain of the Witchard.

No one except for Melody and Sebastian.

***

The naive young couple's families didn't get along so when Melody and Sebastian found themselves with child, they decided to flee from the bickering village nest. The pair wished to get away from wagging tongues and angry elders and start afresh, alone. Each was all the other needed.

Sebastian was handy with an axe and Melody, a fair, fair maiden, handy also with an axe, was not a fan of sunshine, so they rode off and into the forest together on horseback, cart attached, taking with them everything they figured they'd need.

They stopped to rest by a tremendous oak, the tallest, thickest old man of the forest. There, deep within, the giant tree stood out like a beacon, proud father amongst its shorter peers—ash, hawthorn, holly and hazel. Melody wondered around the other side of the great wooden beast and made a fantastical discovery—with excitement in her voice, she beckoned Sebastian over.

Like a desert mirage, there stood the abandoned house. The great oak, landmark that it was, sat on the crest of its garden. The rose-coloured shutters, four chimneys and a half-moon shaped garden, made it appear exactly as foretold. Years of ivy growth climbed up its wood-panelled side,.

They entered it, hand-in-hand. Melody's broad smile told Sebastian it would become their home despite it needing a lot of work. But he agreed—it would save them much time not having to start from scratch.

"It's perfect." Melody pulled her beau from small room to small room. "Bedroom. Bathroom. Kitchen. Front room. Each with its own wood burner for heating and cooking." She cried with happiness and kissed Sebastian passionately. From within her heavy belly, their first child kicked.

"Place your hand, here. Can you feel it?" she said with another smile, one that could light up the darkest part of the forest.

"Yes. Not long now," said Sebastian. The pair set about unpacking and cleaning the inside of their new dwellings.

***

The forest provided plentiful fuel for the fire each evening; mushrooms, nuts, berries and wild rabbit or squirrel kept their bellies full, but with Melody's belly swelling more each day, there came a point at which foraged fruits and trapped meats were no longer satiating her cravings. She wanted bread. *Pastries!* And for bread and pastries, a journey back into the village of Monkton was required. Sebastian went out of the forest for the first time in months, on a lonesome quest for something more substantial to eat.

She bid him farewell and set about her day's task: pulling weeds from the garden path. The *garden could be magnificent by spring,* she thought, *with a little care.* Time combed its skeletal fingers through the treetops and played with the shape of the shadows. It should've been a short gallop, there and back in under an hour, but by sunset, there was no sign of Sebastian's return. Melody became alarmed.

The black cloak of night fast approached. Melody, alone, felt increasingly unsafe. She thumbed and kneaded awkwardly the small of her lower back, massaged her tender bump. *Surely he should be back by now?*

She sat by the fire, her senses sharpened to every bump and hoot the forest gave up. Her anxiety peaked around midnight. Unable to sleep, full of babe, she contemplated puttinging on her hobnail-boots and coat. If she tore down a branch from the oak at the end of her garden path, with enough hessian sack wrapped around its end, she could fix a make-shift torch. With a firestick, she could head out into the night and begin the quest to find her Sebastian. *Has he fallen from his horse? Is my darling hurt? What of the hidden quagmire that loops around the woods?*

In preparation for worst case scenario, she gathered a small medical kit—bandages and balms—in case he was injured. She was ready to set off but let out a sigh of relief when, at last, the front door swung open: her lover had returned.

"Melody." He stumbled towards her, face sallow, eyes bloodshot, owlish, his hair swept like tossed salad. "Melody, darling. Thank heavens. Thought I'd never find you."

"Where've you been?" She peppered him with kisses.

"I've been traipsing the forest for a lifetime of eternities. Couldn't find it. You. The house—" He collapsed with exhaustion onto their bed. "I couldn't find anything, our home. Everything's moved."

***

He'd been searching for hours, retraced his route myriad times. He'd quested into and out of the forest's edge again and again, certain he'd not taken a different path than the one where he'd initially

109

made his departure. It was in this moment of despair that they learnt of the magic of the forest and all that rested—or jumped—within it.

***

The next morning they feasted on the bounty Sebastian had brought back and discussed how to tackle the shifting foundations of their home. They fastened to the giant oak—part and parcel of the property—two strands of golden rope; anchorage of sorts. The string glinted whenever light managed to make its way down through the treetop roof and soupy atmosphere of the forest.

"That should help," they said.

Their firstborn, a son, came along later that day. They named the young babe Sylvain, *'forest dweller'*.

***

Whenever Melody or Sebastian ventured out, they tied the golden cord around their waists to help find their way home. When Sebastian was out chopping and lumbering wood, Melody would spy the taut string stretched out, marking his path, the rope's end looped safely around the huge oak. Sat in her cosy nursing chair looking out of her window, fireside, babe in arms, she would wait and watch at dusk for it to slacken. As rope hit floor, she knew her love was within a stone's throw and her heart had cause to celebrate.

***

For some time they lived happily, reassured by the ropes. Their existence was humble, but by staying within the woods, they remained shielded from endless family feuds. Despite its mysterious abilities to relocate their house, the forest had enchanted them and had—so far—brought them no harm.

***

Several seasons passed. A second babe came along. Sylvain, the eldest, a now toddling boy, became big brother to a girl, a plump dumpling of a thing, still so new, she'd yet to be named.

Now with growing kin, Sebastian found himself making more journeys within the forest for firewood and further afield in search of food. Flour, oil, eggs and sugarcane were available in the village of Monkton. He'd trade for such commodities with bags of kindling.

The wood of the forest had special properties. When chopped, it was a gorgeous flesh shade of peach, it burned slowly and the little smoke it did yield blew out of chimney tops like glittering pinched-pink scarves. The demand for 'Witchard wood' spread. Sebastian found himself gone for several days at a time, chopping and selling.

***

Three days had passed since Sebastian had left for what she beliieved was the last time.. Each day brought with it tremendous jumps—of the house, and in the development of their two young babes. Their eldest, Sylvain, now babbled with almost-words.

Melody was beyond excited. Sebastian was to return that evening. *Thank goodness!* Three days felt like three months, alone with two small babes in the woods.

But she did adore her home amongst the trees. She especially loved the variety of nuts and berries the forest proffered, all of which were delicious. To busy herself while waiting for Sebastian to return, she dedicated her afternoon to exploring the woods for food. She wished to collect a new berry she'd seen but not tasted yet. She'd create something delicious for Sebastian, to celebrate his return: jam perhaps to smother the bread she'd sent him out to buy.

Now, late Autumn, the intriguing plant's tendrils, leaves and berries blanketed thick and velvety the forest floor. Black whilst growing and pink when ripe, the berries were a fair size. She could hold three in her palm at a time. 'Screechberries' they were called, if childhood memories served correctly.

Both babes were strapped to her body, one front, one back, a basket in her hand, and golden string attached to her waist, she travelled through the forest like a nomad. Her youngest slept like a dream through the day, only waking for feeds and changes. *If only she slept so well at night,* Melody would think whilst rocking and nursing the crying wee girl from sundown to sunrise. Sylvain, her eldest, protested about being kept tight in the sling—he was very much awake. He thumped her on her shoulder with pudgy hands, pulled on her hair. She decided to let him down. This slowed her pace considerably but lightened her load and she was in no particular rush.

Sylvain proved to be useful. He, with a chubby index finger, was the first to point out a patch of sweet, ripe fruit. Pink fleshy berries grew in clusters on the ground beneath large, veined, purple leaves. Each berry was composed of two parts and the two parts together resembled pouting, juicy lips.

"Mmmmm," Sylvain hummed and bent down closer to his treasure. "Bewwy."

"Oh Sylvain. Clever boy. Did you just say *berry*? Your first proper word. Berry! Say it again." Melody, proud mother, encouraged her son to find his vocal cords and helped him part back leaves so he could yank free a fruit. "Go ahead, pick one. Try it."

"Bewwy yummy?" he asked, all gummy-grin and spittle. Melody, brimming with pride, nodded at her eldest then glanced down at her second-born who was still swaddled tight, still content, still sleeping pressed firm against her bosom. The little girl's cheeks were as pink as the berries. *Berry* Melody thought. *We shall call you Berry.* Her heart swelled with excitement at the thought of announcing her suggestion to her beloved on his return.

113

Sylvain yanked his first berry free from its stem. The boy jumped back in shock—the firm pluck, berry from stem, released a piercing screech. Even though Melody had an idea of the sound the berry might make, it still took her by surprise.

"Oh my," she laughed softly. Her boy stood stock-still: wide-eyed, muddled somewhere between fear and joy in response to the ear-piercing sound. "That really was quite loud, wasn't it? Here, taste it." She plucked the calyx out from the body of the peculiar fruit and split it in two. The berry, now half a lip, screeched loudly again as it was torn. She passed half to her son. What a cacophony. The pair of them both chuckled this time. In her mouth, rich juices burst free. The berry tasted good. Sylvain chewed, berry-voiced screams released with each chomp of his gums.

Young Sylvain's fingertips and cheeks became smeared with blood-red juices. His maw looked like he'd consumed fresh flesh. Melody tried to wipe him clean with a leaf - to no avail.

They moved around the forest, filling their bellies and the basket until the tiger-stripes of light began to fade and Melody felt the familiar chill of evening in the air. She lifted her eldest up and placed him once more against her tired spine for the return journey. Taut golden thread would lead the way back to their rootless house—who knew where their cottage might now rest?

She started to walk into the rope, hurling great loops of it over her shoulder. Each yank took her a little closer. She paused briefly to rub a little dirt

114

from her eye. When she re-opened her eyes, there, as clear as the nose on her face, sat a second house.

***

This house was different from her own, only half the size. One solitary chimney from which no smoke came at all decorated its roof. It had a garden flourishing with the most beautiful selection of flowers she'd ever seen.

Above the house, through a break in the canopy, the scant light of dusk travelled down, illuminating this strange finding. The garden was truly delightful, vibrant and buzzing with colourful petals and fruits and vegetables in all manner of shapes, shades and sizes,. Bumbling bees darted in and out of hollyhock trumpets, spiral tendrils of pumpkin wound up and around cane frames, bushes filled with myriad berries in all shades of the rainbow sparkled even in the dim light like jewels at Melody and her babes. Enthralled—for her own garden had yielded nothing but dirt and stubborn weeds—Melody placed her overflowing basket of berries at her feet and straightened her back. Could she creep a little closer to explore the bountiful garden display?

"Oh my. I wonder—" she said but both babes were fast asleep.

"Clear off."

A voice. From the cottage window?

Melody looked to the house and saw in an instant at the window a flash-frost of snow-white hair. From within the mess of tangles, beetle-black eyes glinted out at her, or so she thought. But then, in a blink of an eye, the window became again a dark, empty square. Her heart bashed. She turned around immediately, pulled on her golden rope and instructed her legs to run.

"Clear off. Get out of my forest. Unless—" the ancient voice came loud again, stealing her full attention. It paused. "Unless... you have something for me?" The voice sounded needy, pained. Was this a person who required help?

Melody turned back around to face the property—she was scared but she was also kind. If there was someone else living in the forest, if she and Sebastian did indeed have a neighbour, then wouldn't it be best to try and be 'neighbourly'? Try and get along? She wasn't sure if she believed in magic anyway, or curses, or witches and wizards. She'd often wondered about the night when Sebastian claimed the house had moved—had perhaps proud Sebastian gotten badly lost instead, been too embarrassed to admit it? Maybe her home hadn't shifted one inch at all.

A motherly instinct to protect her young burned deep within her gut but her legs were dog-tired and, alas, refused to respond. Whoever this person was, whatever this person was, if it wished her harm, she feared she would not be able to out run it anyway. *We've made ourselves a home here. No more running away.*

"I've berries," she said. Her voice came out quieter, more broken, than she'd hoped. She cleared her throat and spoke again. "Would you like some?"

116

Again, the white mass of hair appeared at the window, beneath it, a cape of tessellated dry leaves. The sight was enough to make Melody suck in a sharp breath and take back several steps.

"Does it look like I need berries, girl?" The words, like frosty stalactites, spiked out through the gaps between the old timbers of the cottage's walls. The words barked up Melody's spine, icing every vertebra as they travelled.

Melody panicked. What else did she have to offer? Other than the very clothes she was wearing, the golden rope wrapped in reams hung over her shoulder and her precious babes strapped to her body, she had nothing left on her to give.

"What do you need?"

A long moment passed in which not a sound was made. Then, the being spoke again: "You've a young man, haven't you? I've seen him taking more than his fair share; carrying wood out of the forest. My forest. Selling it to villagers. Through the trees, I see everything."

Melody spun around faster than a weathercock on a windy day, tangling herself in rope, certain she'd heard something creeping up behind her. A branch snapping underfoot? Was something else with her, in the woods outside of the pop-up cottage? From the corner of her eye, did an old knot in a thick trunk wink at her? A squirrel scarpered up the same tree. *Must have been the squirrel.* Her heart banged at triple speed. Her arms twisted around her core, one hand cupped firmly on each of her babes' heads.

"Yes. Sebastian. Love of my life," she replied, petrified this being with hair as white as an erased memory, with eyes black as death, might have been after her precious Sebastian.

"Take take take. It's all anyone ever does from my forest."

"I'm sorry," said Melody, her arms holding the string and squeezing both of her children tighter than she'd ever done before.

"I am in need of something actually. From you. Spells and curses only stretch so far. I'm weak in strength, for I'm old—almost as old as the forest itself. I am old and I am cold."

"Please. Is there anything I can do? Sebastian— he'll be back soon. He can help too."

In response, rather than anger bursting out from within the cottage, she heard sobbing. And with the sobbing, the boughs of many a great tree around her seemed to sag, as if weeping with their Witchard. The being spoke again.

"Bring me chopped wood and you can remain in the forest, I'm too old to drag it myself. These are tired hands. And your husband—he must take less. It's not sustainable to reap more than you sow."

"I understand," Melody looked down at her youngest. She appeared to be rousing from sleep, soon keen to feed at her breast, no doubt. She smoothed a wisp of blonde hair from her baby girl's face. "I must return home now. We'll make amends, I assure you. I'll be back with wood. We've plentiful spare."

"Of course."

Melody looked back to the window. There was no longer any sign of anyone there. Its voice had retracted to a whisper which was almost lost to the

118

gentle evening breeze: "Follow your golden string, girl. Follow your golden string."

Melody crept up the Witchard's garden path, under the arch of beautiful flora and tied her golden rope to the knocker of the front door. She planned to return home, deposit her harvest, fetch wood and bring it to the Witchard before sunset; she'd enough time before Sebastian was due to return. She'd need to follow the rope to relocate the mysterious cottage.

***

Melody made it back home. She emptied her berries into a bowl, nursed her baby girl, then filled the basket with chunks of wood. Once more, with her two babies strapped to her, she set out and followed the golden rope all the way back to the Witchard's cottage.

She wanted to appease the Witchard, ensure their place within the woods was safe and then she wished to return home. The fire needed stoking until it roared, until it became angry enough to warm up her home so her baby girl would doze. She had jam to make.

Moments later, with the firewood stacked neatly to the side of the Witchard's door, she undid the loop of golden string from the door handle and started returning home.

"Thank you, girl. For giving back to the forest. The forest may thank you, in due turn." The voice broke through the silence of dusk. "Then again, it may not." Melody's pace down the Witchard's path quickened. She noticed small mounds of earth dotted in between the beautiful, fruitful flora, each pierced with a makeshift inverted cross of dried branches.

It was as if the creepy being could hear her thoughts: "Dead creatures, dear girl. Found, dead creatures of the forest. Nothing to fear." Yet fear did indeed quicksilver through Melody's veins. The Witchard's voice boomed once more: "Rot. Decay. Nature's loop. Keeps my soil fertile." Melody cheetahed down the last few yards of path.

A distance away, her breath coming hard and fast, her babies heavy, her legs weak for it had been a long and arduous day, she braved a turn to look back behind her. The Witchard's house with its beautiful gardens could no longer be seen. Only a hazy trail of glitter-pink smoke billowed in the distance, snaking its way between and around the skeletal branches of the deciduous or dead parts of the forest. Melody wondered if she might ever see her ominous neighbour again. She hoped not.

***

On returning home, she fed her small babe then laid her down in a basket in the living room and pulled out a sack of paper and pencils for Sylvain to scribble with until bed time. Children sleeping or occupied, she went about starting up the fire: night was a nearby visitor.

With the fire lit and Sylvain's cheeks aglow and Berry, full of milk, settled peacefully in her basket, Melody went out to the kitchen to start preparing jam. Hundreds of berries needed to be de-leafed, split and scrubbed and as she did so, a cacophony of fitful, piercing screams and wails filled the air. Purple-pink juices stained her fingers as she plucked and squeezed. Such noisy berries from such a quiet wood.

***

The knock at the door startled Melody. She dropped her knife. She dried her hands on her apron and went to turn the front door handle.

No-one.

All she could see was a still-taut golden rope anchored to the oak and the creep of night descending on their scrubby clearing of a garden. Who could it have been? A cold breeze slapped her fire-warmed cheeks with a sobering clunk. An owl whooped, flapped its wings and took flight from somewhere. Her heart missed a beat. No-one there but there, at her feet was the strangest of items.

She picked it up so she could see it clearly. In her hands, cold and heavy, was the most peculiar carving of a face of sorts, made from a length of forest wood, the same length and weight as one of the logs she'd not long ago gifted to The Witchard.

The chiselled face felt soft beneath the stroke of her finger tips, although, it was not a friendly face. Quite the opposite; the whittled visage featured an expression of pure terror and it bore a likeness to her dearest: it was a carving of Sebastian's head.

Stuck tight to the foot-high statue of her love's face staring up at her were two eyes of polished obsidian, as black and as bottomless as the midnight forest. Real, ghost-white hair fell from the crown of its head all a tangle, all in knots, attached firmly to the wood; hair just like the Witchard's own.

On realising the similarity to Sebastian, she dropped the piece in shock. A pulse of vomit throbbed in her throat.

The carving was quite repulsive and smelt a little of damp and musty leaves. She lifted it again, looking for certainty over where it might have come from. She saw a word etched onto its base: 'Thank you'. The Witchard. *Must be a gift in exchange for the wood*; a piece of which, it seemed to be shaped from. A grotesque and unwanted gift, but a gift nonetheless. She carried the piece into the house and placed it in the corner of the front room.

"Mumma, s'that?" Sylvain asked, his first clear sentence, but Melody, distracted by the odd delivery, shooed him away from the carving and encouraged him to return to his art.

***

Melody stoked the fire with a further log and then returned to the kitchen where she did the same again. Smoke spilled out from two of four chimneys and Sebastian, closing in, could see two pink, sparkling ribbons in the distance. He was following his golden rope.

Melody set about stewing her screaming berries. There was still jam to prepare. Didn't they wince in audible pain as the bottom of the cast iron pan sat upon the hot top of the wood burner?

122

Melody felt a tap on the back of her leg. Young Sylvain stood behind her as she stood by the stove. "What is it, sweetpea?" she asked. Her young child's face was full of woe.

"Don't like it." Sylvain said. The child kicked dirt from the floor with his foot.

"Oh darling, neither do I. Turn it around. Face it away from you. Please let me continue, Father will be back shortly. Watch for him from the front room window."

The child skulked back to the front room. Melody dipped her finger into the sweet 'n' soupy mixture and tasted a sample. "Too sour," she said and wiped a sticky finger on her tatty pink kitchen rag. She tossed this dirtied tea-towel over her shoulder and added more sugar. The berry yelps seemed to be growing louder as they meshed to sugary mush. A moment later, the familiar tap of Sylvain at her leg came again. "What is it, Sylvain? I'm nearly done, then I'll come and colour too, whilst we wait for Father."

"S'howwible. Don't like iyy." The boy sulked, stamped his foot. Melody crouched down to face her son. She understood. She too had felt that way when holding the odd carving. Did it have some sort of power to it, an evil force? Cursed? She still wasn't sure she believed in such craft, but she promised Sylvain she'd be in shortly to deal with the situation.

"Drape this over it, darling. Out of sight is out of mind." She passed him the tatty, berry-juice stained cloth. One corner of Sylvain's mouth lifted slightly. "And take a few of these, to tide over your hunger." She handed him a small bowl of berries. Head hung low, he toddled back through the partition door and into the front room at his mother's direction.

Melody continued to stir her jam. Sebastian would be over the moon. Over the racket the noisy preserve was making in the hot pan, she heard Sylvain shouting out from the front room. "Mummy, no likey. Howwible face."

Melody, both impressed with her son's language development and torn between finishing her task and quelling the young boy's concerns shouted back. "Oh darling. I'll be in shortly. One moment." She poured the hot, sweet, thick liquid into a jar, careful not to spill a drop and glad to screw the lid on to leave the raucous berries to settle. "If it's really bothering you, I'll be with you in a shake of a lamb's tail. We shall simply chuck it on the fire, be done with it."

The forest was darkening rapidly. Melody glanced out of the kitchen window at the great oak. Blackness, but her attuned eyes could make out the position of the golden rope. It lay flat on the path. Sebastian would soon be home. Joy. A rush of excitement dashed up to her heart and she dashed into the front room and towards the front door.

"Mumma. Mumma." Sylvain was tugging at her leg. "No more scary." He smiled at her and she bent down to wipe berry juice from his cheeks with a lick of her finger the way mothers do. She swooped him up and rested him against the bone of her hip before moving towards the door, certain she could hear the crackle of boot and hoof on dried bracken in the distance. How glad she'd be to have her family together as one again. Was that him, a movement she saw through the window?

Sylvain pointed to the carving which sat upright in its corner, facing into the front room. "S'at, Mumma?" he asked and pointed again at the oddity, a quizzical look on his young face.

Melody froze. She swore she'd instructed her son to turn it. Had it moved back around by itself? Another noise outside. Her vision flitted from the window to the door of the wood burner, which had been swung wide open. The flames inside the cast iron box were roaring, bright and hot as hell. From its white-orange maw trailed the end of a berry-pink tea-towel.

"Why is the—" Melody placed Sylvain down, her eyes, wide open, not moving from the trail of pink towel. Her chest puffed high, her lungs held onto a full volume of air.

Sebastian pushed open the front door to his home. "Melody, my darling—"

Melody looked at her husband then rushed to the basket in which she had laid down her darling daughter babe to rest, only to find it empty; babe gone. She turned and yanked back out the half burnt tea-towel and screamed at the fire. Her terror shouted out louder than a forest full of bursting berries. When Sebastian too understood what had happened, his face became the spit of the Witchard's carving.

Backwards Lonesome

Rickey Rivers Jr

1.

Marlon had dreamed of space for years. In childhood he had toys of spacemen, spaceships and aliens. His mother encouraged his enthusiastic interest. Marlon loved space. He had always wanted to be elsewhere. The idea of space haunted his mother. She wasn't afraid before he left her.

***

There was a knock at the door and Marie rose from the couch to answer. She was wrapped in a blanket belonging to her son. She left the blanket behind and went to the front door. She opened it and saw a man in uniform.

"Morning," said the man.

"Morning," she said.

"Marie Booth?"

"Yes?"

"Ma'am, I have some terrible news."

In a way she knew what was next. In a way she expected it. "Go on," she said. "Tell me the news."

***

In therapy she relayed the story, blaming herself. "I should have said no."

"No one is to blame."

"Someone is, someone always is."

"Accidents happen."

"They lost contact, everyone's assumed to be dead. What a terrible thing to tell a mother."

Her therapist nodded. She had no words.

***

Marlon held up his tiny figures. "See, this is the alien and this is the space man."

"Oh, I see."

"And this spaceship came from Earth!"

"Can Earth make spaceships?"

"In the future they can!"

She laughed.

"It's true, Momma. When we fight the aliens we'll take their ships and learn how they make them."

"Oh, I see."

"I can't wait."

"You can't wait for what?"

"For space, I wanna go there. I wanna be a spaceman."

"You have to finish school first."

"I know Momma." His eyes lit up.

She enjoyed his imagination.

***

127

"Ma'am, I'm very sorry about what happened. Marlon was a good man, a good friend."

"Who are you?" she asked, hearing a voice beside her, feeling a hand on her shoulder.

"I'm Scott. I worked with Marlon."

"Oh? Why didn't you go up?"

"I… I work in the labs, ma'am, transfer."

"Oh?"

By the time she realized her cruelty, the man had said his goodbyes. Marie Booth stood staring at all the people in black walking across the perfectly cut gravesite.

At this time she wondered if tears meant anything or if they were something people did when they didn't know what else to do.

***

"Marlon, listen to me-"

"I have been. I'm in the program. This is what happens. I'm gonna train for six months. It'll be all right."

Marie Booth went searching for the words. "J-just think about it."

"Ma, you already knew about this."

"I didn't know you'd go into space. I didn't want that."

Marlon shook his head. "You knew, though, that it could happen."

"But I didn't want it to."

"You know what it means to me. You know I'll be fine. The equipment, the shuttle, everything always gets checked, double checked and triple checked. Everything's gonna be fine."

"I know, Marlon. I know and I love you so much, I just don't want anything to -you know, you know."

He hugged her. "I know you're scared, Ma. We did a simulation, it scared me too. But I wouldn't go up there if it hadn't been done before. We know other folks went. I know I can do it too."

She buried her face into his chest and muffled the curses within.

***

Marie Booth spent time with friends and family, trying her best to be normal. She grew tired of answering questions. She loved talking of him and his accomplishments, but doing so with him not even on the same planet made her sadder and sadder. She didn't know where he was physically and the thought of that worried her. So when his name was brought up she would change the subject. It didn't make sense to talk about someone unless you knew for certain that they were safe and sound.

At one point she spent time looking at his old toys, report cards, photos and anything that reminded her of him before she decided that doing so was pointless. She told herself that it would be more productive to get her mind off of him and pick up hobbies instead, catch up on television shows, read, anything. She told herself this would help. So she kept her mind occupied. Her therapist told her how important it was.

***

There it stood, high in the sky, the white shuffle, the orange tank gleaming in the sunlight. Spectators came from all over, some cheering, taking photos and Marie Booth stood among the crowd, rigid and worried.

The rockets would blast and the smoke cloud would follow.

He had waved to her and she had waved back. But she was uneasy.

"Be careful," she said. But no one heard that.

***

One day she stood in his old room and thought of burning it all, the old toys, the old bed, everything that remained until nothing remained.

"Stupid," she said, kicking an old spaceship, regretting the action and recovering the pieces which hit against the wall.

She picked up a plastic spaceman and squeezed so tight it hurt. The pristine comic collection with aliens, robots and other oddities stared back at her, shaming her. Finally, she broke down and curled up on the floor, weeping into the carpet which still had his smell.

***

She gave everything to her therapist, all the words she kept inside.

130

"I know I shouldn't feel like that."

"Anger is natural. Emotion is natural."

Marie Booth shook her head. "I encouraged him so much. I shouldn't have."

"You didn't do anything wrong."

Anger rose within. "Say something else, anything else."

"A child will always find a path. The teachings of a parent will always be with the child, but the parent can't control the path."

"…I wanted to be with him."

"A child has to walk alone, eventually."

Marie sighed.

"The lessons of the past will always be here." The therapist pointed to her head. "You can't foresee the future, good or bad. You've done your job. There is no blame."

"But I'm the one-"

"Never regret encouragement. This is no blame."

Marie took a deep breath.

***

She felt trapped in the lonely house with all the old stuff. Some nights she woke up screaming. Unhealthy thoughts became common place, but she always shook them away. She was haunted. The past had decided the future and she had no input. All the hobbies and TV shows meant nothing. Something always reminded her of him. Someone was always an age she remembered.

131

There was a knock at the door. Marie Booth rose from the couch, leaving his blanket behind. She opened the door and saw him standing there. This was a man she grew to hate. He wore a spacesuit and helmet. The helmet reflected anger.

"What do you want?"

The spacemen lifted his arms and pulled off his helmet. This man was her son.

"Hey, Momma"

Marie Booth caught herself from stumbling backwards. It wasn't true. It couldn't be true. Yet there he stood, familiar, but not.

"Marlon?" she said.

The space man nodded. His space suit was charred and his helmet was cracked. Underneath it all she saw it was him.

Her body shook and tears came. She wanted to hug him, but warmth came from direction. Then a smell followed. And the truth began to crawl and wrap itself around reality.

"Son," she said, for the first time in a long time and something balled up in her throat.

"I'm okay, Momma." The spaceman stood there, barely there, swaying, a scarecrow from a dream.

"Is it really you?"

"It's me." His skin was jerky, tough and crackled.

A slow scan of him told the story. Marie Booth saw the flaws. He was not him, only he as he once was. This spaceman was an image, an image of longing, a nightmare reality. Her mind told her this and as it did clumps began to fall. They fell off the spacesuit, then off the charred skin of the spaceman.

"Momma, what's wrong?"

The spaceman's nose began to slide and his ears followed and his eyes became smoky in their sockets.

She turned away from this scene, the sight unbearable.

"You have to leave," she said. Not wanting that, but deciding that doing so was right. He needed to leave.

"Momma, I'm tired." His voice was low, weakened.

"So rest, you have to rest, just somewhere else."

"Momma," his voice went to ages prior. "I'm so tired."

Marie Booth slunk back into her home and shut the door behind her. Marlon's helmet fell to the ground and shattered, what was left of his spacesuit crumpled. And Marlon's ashes blew in the autumn wind.

For this act, Marie Booth thought herself heartless.

***

But time went on. She kept talk of the visitor away from her therapist and over time she saw improvement. The memories, the pain of the past didn't hurt as it once had. Slowly Marie got back to herself and her anger lessened. She took all his toys and bagged them up. Weeks became months. Life seemed to normalize.

She never saw the spaceman again. She never saw Marlon again. Joyous moments became a blanket of peace. Mother and son able to move on, all regrets laid to rest.

An Evening Stroll Along The Tracks

Brian Barnett

Kevin and Will walked in a single file trying to balance on the steel rail of the abandoned railroad track that ran along the outside of town. They wanted to go the adventurous route home from Evan's house. Both were full of pizza and it was getting dark.

"Why haven't we ever gone this way home before?" asked Will. He was shakily keeping his balance behind Kevin who seemed steadier.

"Probably because my parents told me not to."

"I guess that's a good enough reason." Will's foot slipped and he waved his arms like a windmill in a tornado but he eventually lost his balance and dropped to the ground.

"Man, I told you I'd go longer than you."

"Yeah, yeah. I just slipped."

"Dude, look up there! There's a tunnel!" Kevin jumped from the rail to the ground.

"Awesome!"

The boys jogged along the tracks, passing tall weeds growing up and around the old rotted oak sleepers. The tunnel seemed to loom larger the closer they got. It was dark inside and getting darker by the minute as the sun had nearly dipped below the line of buildings behind them.

They paused at the edge of it, both in awe. It was maybe a hundred yards in length and maybe twelve or so feet wide. A cool breeze chilled their shins.

Once they stepped inside the air felt cooler. The shade and the gentle breeze was a nice change from the muggy summer weather. Even though it was evening, it was still rather warm out.

The sound of the old packed gravel crunching under their feet reverberated off the walls of the tunnel. It was so loud compared to their otherwise quiet walk before making it to the tunnel. They couldn't even hear the katydids anymore. Only crunching and their own breathing.

"Hey, what if there are bats in here?" Will asked.

"I don't know. Maybe one will bite you and you'll become a vampire."

"Don't bats have rabies?"

"I don't know. Probably not all of them. But I heard you have to get shots in your stomach if you get bit."

Will slouched a bit, just in case.

"I think I'd be more worried about bumping into some hobo."

"A hobo?"

"Yeah, you know, some guy drifting from town to town, catching trains and stuff."

"But these tracks haven't been used in, like, forever."

"All the more reason to worry about hobos. Can you imagine? By now he'd be starving and probably half-crazy if there was one in here."

"Stop it, Kevin. There's no hobos in here. Good grief."

Will caught himself looking over his shoulder. Just in case. The end of the tunnel they entered was a good distance behind them now. The orange sunset had turned to more of a purple. The buildings in the distance were more shadowed and it was harder to make out their features.

"Yeah, you're right. I'll stop. But what if it was haunted?"

"There's no such thing as ghosts."

"Who told you that? Your parents? Parents always say stuff like that."

"No. I mean, yes, they did, but I just don't believe in ghosts. I'm not a little kid."

"Well if one of those abandoned hobos died in here, maybe he's just waiting for a train to show up. If one never does, I guess he's just lingering here in the tunnel."

"Kevin, this is the reason why I'm the only one who will hang out with you."

Kevin laughed. "Evan hangs out with me too."

"Yeah because he doesn't have to listen to your stupid made up stories all day."

"I think he's scared, folks!" Keven announced as if sharing with an audience.

"No I'm not. I'm annoyed."

Kevin raised his hands, wiggled his fingers in a spooky gesture, and made ghostly sounds "w0o-oo-oo-oo-oo".

"Finally, jeez."

Kevin barely noticed that they had exited the tunnel. It was already quite a bit darker than it was

137

just a few minutes ago when they had entered. Despite the darkness, it was still muggy out. The katydids were as loud as ever.

"We better get home soon. My parents will ground me if I come home late again," he said.

"Yeah, same here." Will agreed.

They quickened their pace along the tracks. Fortunately, they lived next door to one another and they were maybe another fifteen minutes away from getting home.

After a few yards, they saw a light ahead. It was bobbing around as if someone was carrying a flashlight.

"There's one of those hobos I was talking about."

"Shut up, Kevin. He might hear you."

"The hobo?"

"He's not a hobo, stop it."

Neither boy could make out features of the person carrying the light. But the closer they got, they could tell it wasn't a flashlight, it was an old-style kerosene lantern. "Are you two crazy?" a man's voice called.

The boys froze.

"Get off those tracks!" the man waved his hand, gesturing them to step aside. But by now the tracks were on a steep hill. There was no safe place to climb down until they passed where the man was standing.

"We will!" Will answered. "I'm sorry. We didn't know we weren't supposed to be on the tracks. We didn't tear anything up."

138

The man continued walking toward them. "'Didn't know you weren't...'" the man stammered. "Boys, are you thick or something?"

The boys started to walk back toward the tunnel, keeping an eye on the man with the lantern.

"This guy is weird." Kevin whispered.

"No kidding."

"Where do you two think you're going? You stay right there!"

"Uh, we were just going home. We'll just go right now." Kevin said as he turned and ran. "Come on, Will!"

Will quickly turned and followed Kevin on instinct. He wasn't sure why he was running but it seemed a safe bet considering some weird guy with an old gas lantern was yelling at them. Who carries a lantern? Will didn't recognize the man's voice. Maybe it was an old hobo after all.

Within seconds the loud crunching of rocks was deafening inside the tunnel. Not long after they entered a third pair of feet were crunching behind them.

"I said get off the tracks!" the man yelled. His voice was booming in the tunnel, which only made the boys' legs pump harder to get through it.

The boys were most the way through the tunnel when they heard something that chilled them to their cores. A not-so-distant train whistle sounded.

"Oh my god!" Will yelled.

"I thought these tracks were abandoned!" yelled Kevin.

"Get off the tracks!" yelled the man. He had gained some ground on them.

The train whistle sounded again. Closer.

Just ahead, they saw a massive black train engine with black smoke pouring from the smokestack. A single round blinding headlight drew closer as the engine barreled toward them, rumbling the ground under their feet. It was impossible to hear anything else in the tunnel.

The boys reached the end of the tunnel, ran a few feet clear of the tracks, and tumbled into the patch of grass next to the brick buildings. The train blew through the tunnel, carrying car after car after car. The wind in their wake tugged at the boys' shirts. The sound echoed off the buildings behind them. The smell of burning coal burned their noses and made their eyes water. Finally, the last car disappeared into the tunnel.

The ground had stopped vibrating but it made little difference. Both boys were shaking from their near death experience. Will could taste his pizza again in the back of his throat.

"What about that guy!" Will asked.

"Oh man." Kevin nervously ran his hands through his hair. "There's no way he made it out alive. There's just no way."

"Well we have to see, just in case we can help him or something."

"Alright, dude, but it might be pretty bad."

The boys made their way back to the track and braced themselves for what they might see in the tunnel. Maybe the man could have pressed himself to one side and the train may have missed him. But both boys knew better.

But when they looked into the tunnel, there was nothing. The man wasn't there. Neither was his lantern. The boys traced the tracks all the way, as far as they could see and there was no train either.

Kevin wiped the cold sweat off his brow. "Man, I told you it was haunted."

Mesmerized in the Glaring Randomness of Chance

Dona Fox

Thrown to the side of the road. Stunned. I listened to my breath in the otherwise silent night. Wheezing. My body steaming. So warm, finally, warm. One leg shook, as if trying to rise. I needed to find my child.

***

My roaming began in 1964, in the Cajon Pass, just off Highway 138 up on Rail Road property. Or maybe it started that morning when I pried Brandy's hand off my chest and tucked it under the covers. I smiled as she grumbled, "stay in bed, Jack."

She turned away, leaving in her wake the scent of beer and stale cigarette smoke so I had an idea where she'd been last night. Again. I was thankful she always managed to find her way home and back into our bed.

I tucked a strand of hair behind her ear and bent to kiss her cheek then, instead, I wet a cloth to wash the dried vomit off her lips. That was so Lili wouldn't see it when she came in to wake her mom. Once again, I wondered if I was staying with Brandy to make up for the shame I felt for my mother's death.

142

Brandy shook me off, "don't wake Lili," she mumbled.

But Lili wasn't asleep. She came padding out, barefoot, in mismatched pajamas—fairies on the top and space ships on the bottom. "I'm hungry. Where's my cereal?"

I wanted to get on the road, then up by the tracks to the ties I'd contracted with the railroad to pick up. I needed to be back home before the promised snowstorm set in.

I jerked the cereal off the shelf, plopped the box on the table along with a bowl and spoon, then yanked open the fridge–no milk. I meant to stop by the Gas & Go for a carton last night, but then I thought there'd be time to pick the milk up on my way home this morning. Obviously, that hadn't worked out.

"When I was a kid, I put water on mine. Have you ever tried that?"

"Ick." She shook her dark curls.

I must have looked pretty pathetic, leaning down into the near-empty fridge. But I'd frozen as I thought again about my mother. Now I know she'd been half-drunk that last day of her life when we'd gone to the S&P Grocery to get milk for my cereal.

Now Lili was next to me peering into the fridge; she put her hand on my cheek, "it's okay, Daddy, I like it best like this." She took a handful out of the box and ate it dry, "this is my favorite way." She smiled. Her teeth were red from the dye in the heart-shaped cereal. I hugged her.

"I'm leaving right now. You need to go back to bed until your mom gets up."

143

"No." She gave me her gray-eyed stare, just like her mother's, as she stuffed another handful of hearts into her mouth.

"You can take the cereal to bed with you," I whispered, pulling her to me, tickling her gently, anything to diffuse that cold stare.

"No way," she giggled, dragging the last word out through the stain on her teeth.

"How about tee-vee?" I mumbled into her hair, just for the smell of her—the sunshine, the baby shampoo, the pillowcase that needed changing.

"How 'bout I go with you? Please?" she wheedled as she hugged the cereal box to her body, the cardboard heart on the cover right over her own.

I looked at the clock. Sure, we could get back before her mom was up.

"Okay, bring your cereal and wear your fuzzy boots and the bright red jacket."

She wrinkled her nose, "not the red one?"

"Yes. Or you stay home."

"Okay. Thank you, Daddy!" She ran, bouncing, and came back wearing the jacket, still clutching the box of her favorite cereal.

On second thought, I'd better tell Brandy my plans—when my mom couldn't find me in the S&P grocery store, they tell me she became frantic. She'd ran out into the street crying my name.

"You wait right there." I held a warning hand out to Lili; she bounced up and down tossing cereal in the general direction of her mouth.

"Brandy," I sat on the edge of the bed and shook her shoulder; she pushed me away, "listen to me; I'm leaving and I'm taking Lili. Right now. Do you understand?"

"What the hell!" suddenly wide-awake she rose from the bed like Leviathan from the deep, knocking the lamp and old bottles of partially finished beer from the nightstand, her blood-shot eyes bulging from the sockets. She reached for my face with her nails, "You're not leaving me and you're sure as hell not taking my baby!"

"Whoa. Easy, Brandy. I'm just taking her up the hill with me; we'll be back by supper."

She wilted onto me, sobbing. "I know I haven't been the best mother and I haven't been the best wife. Please don't ever take my baby; don't you leave me and don't take my baby. I'll be better. I'll stay home from now on; I'll even make dinner tonight."

Should I have woke her or not? Either way I would have ended up the bad guy.

"Okay, Brandy, you go back to sleep and don't worry, I'm just taking her up on the mountain with me and we'll be back before supper. I'll see you then, Honey." I leaned down and kissed her. She was asleep before I could get the covers tucked around her. She might or she might not remember this conversation but I wouldn't be expecting the smell of a homecooked meal when I came home hungry.

I found Lili under her bed.

"You can't run and hide every time something scares you, Lili. Next time, come to me, okay?"

"But—"

"No 'buts,' you always come to me." I put my index finger on her mouth.

"Okay, Daddy."

Highway 138 was slushy with last night's snow. I was early enough that the trucks hadn't risen from their nightly hibernation to begin the perilous trek from the top of the Pass. They'd perform intricate maneuvers, much like a tango, as they jockeyed down the steep grades of the mountain.

Apparently, one brave driver had cut out early on his own. I was grateful for his enthusiasm; he'd left dark gray tire tracks for me to follow through the silent world of blue snow and sky.

My old Jeep Willys bounced as I drove off Highway 138 to where I was headed to pick up my load of railroad ties. I was on my own with no more tracks to follow when I spotted Forestry Road 3N45.

We bounced over a couple of railroad crossings; I looked over at Lili. She was sound asleep clutching her cereal box. Her dark lashes fluttered and her eyes quivered beneath the lids; I prayed my daughter always had beautiful dreams— that I could somehow give that to her.

The access road was marked only by the fact no brush grew on it; I knew, like the Forestry Road, there was dirt beneath the snow. Finally, we were on the narrow right of way, it was only about eighty feet wide and a challenge to make out under the snow.

When I exited the truck, I closed the door gently to not wake Lili. I took in a deep breath of the icy air and stretched. I was tall and lanky; my legs were like poles, not only thin but long—growing up, no foster homes wouldn't have me, said the state didn't send them enough money to feed me or to pay for the ever longer pants needed to keep pace with my phenomenal growth. My legs were strong due to the fact I often walked all night, worrying about my wife.

My arms were well muscled. I was up to the task of loading a dozen railroad ties into my pickup.

I've spent a lot of time at this altitude in an attempt to be closer to my father, wondering what he was looking for, thinking it was my fault he was up here so often that he wouldn't have been consorting with the ghosts of the Pass if my mother was still alive. He disappeared in the mountains. They found his body ravaged by the wildlife—wolves, then the ravens.

Mother always said he would pay a price when he brought that wolf cub home. But the pup was alive in his arms so I could see no harm in what he'd done. It was my mother that made the stew. I wouldn't eat it.

Now up on the summit my lungs felt clean as I breathed in the pure, icy air. It was a beautiful day, but real cold at the top of the Pass. The snow was headed our way, closer than I'd expected. I'd better get a move on; there'd be time enough to count my blessings later, a whole lifetime.

The railroad guy had pulled out a dozen ties for me; I hefted a couple, they weighed close to 200

147

pounds each. Two more looked closer to 300, so I knew it would be pushing it with the snow to take all of them today.

Many strange things happen around Cajon Pass, some caused by the horrific events of the long ago. Horse stealing raids raced through right where I stood, leaving the scent of sweat and fear hanging in the air decades later.

Cajon was often the final site for friction between the Mountain Men, the early explorers and the people with a rightful claim to this land. The dead from those events were left exposed to the weather where they were picked over by wild animals and, often, each other, then abandoned to rot into the ground.

Those who died ignobly in the Pass were still tethered to the earth in un-graves where hell-smoke rose in thin spirals to this day, marking shadows of the people on the ground. Sometimes the smoke hissed out of the dirt like a scream from hell.

Heck, even the folks escaping the dust bowl thought they'd found a safe place just down the mountain until the locals lit into them and many ran up here to die.

But the strangest was the braying of the mules. It was a mournful sound that cut right through me, 'specially knowing they'd been dead for over a hundred years; ever since that Santa Fe train came through a snowstorm in a heavy fog and caught the unfortunate beasts under its cowcatcher. I'd heard them a lot but I'd never seen the mangy animals walking dead like some people had.

I could hear the mules braying today and saw the thin streams of smoke hissing up through cracks in the snow's crust as if bodies screamed to be found. I was sorry I'd brought Lili to this haunted, hellish place; I'd work fast and get home.

I grew even more uneasy when I heard a motor revving in the distance. The sound of other humans close by troubled me; I couldn't imagine why anyone would be up here at this time of year. In better weather, further down the mountain, tourists panned for gold or looked for the San Andreas Fault but I wasn't used to seeing or hearing anyone else this far out here in the snow—it was too early in the day and too cold for four wheelers.

I checked on Lili again and draped my jacket over her. I could work faster without the extra encumbrance of the coat. The engine sounds were getting closer.

A greedy thought flashed through my mind— These railroad ties belonged to me. Well, they did. It was a simple fact. I needed these last few ties to finish shoring up the retaining wall behind our trailer so the hill wouldn't come down on us with the spring thaw. I needed these ties for my family's safety.

I was working up a sweat when I could tell the vehicle was headed straight toward us. Not yet on high alert, I wiped the moisture from my face and waited to see who it was; maybe it was only the railroad man making sure I was the legitimate owner of the ties. I had the paper in my front shirt pocket that said 'Jack Doran'-if it wasn't soaked

149

with my sweat-so I'd welcome his arrival, someone looking out for me.

The stranger pulled up behind my Jeep, effectively blocking me from a simple exit. His vehicle showed no official insignia. Not the Forest Service. Not the Rail Road.

When he jumped out of the cab of his pickup, I saw that he wasn't wearing an official uniform either and not only was he moving more aggressively than necessary when no words had been exchanged, but he also had a good forty pounds on me. He was younger and his arms were longer. Advantages. Should it come to that.

I didn't see anyone else in his cab or hiding in the back of his pickup. In the sudden silence as he tipped his head and made as if to circle me, I didn't hear any other vehicles approaching. It was just me and him and his extra forty pounds. And Lili, hopefully sleeping in the cab of my Jeep.

"I been thinkin' those were my railroad ties," he squinted as he stared into my eyes, "and I'm here to pick them up." Now that he was close, I saw that he had watery eyes, a gray beard that framed his face, and huge yellow canines—and a long, wolfish head—just like the glimpse I'd had of the man in the gray sedan that ran down my mom outside the S&P Grocery.

His scent was strong, musty, and unmistakable, like something I'd never smelled before and could never forget. A combination of wet animal, body grease, dry hunger, and aching greed.

I took two steps back; probably a stupid thing to do in this kind of confrontation. At the same

150

time, I raised one palm down toward him and used the other hand, fingers splayed, to reach carefully into my shirt pocket, "I have the proper paperwork. I negotiated the acquisition of these ties with the railroad and, you can see this proves my rightful claim—"

"What the hell does all that gibberish mean! I'm about to get something' that'll prove mine—my rightful claim!" Laughing, he jumped into his truck and drove away. I thought he'd left.

He must have seen something I hadn't seen.

A flash of red disappearing through the brush?

I went back to the Jeep and opened the lockbox. I strapped on my sidearm and finished piling the ties into my truck. Looking back, I should have settled for what I'd loaded at that point and gone home; no physical property is worth a life, no amount of railroad ties, not even the home they were meant to save. But I continued to work and as I worked, I realized I should have chased after him and shot him for the physical threat and to protect my daughter, not for the railroad ties and what they represented to us. We were in mortal danger. But all that would have done no good. It was already too late.

Finally done, I threw my gloves in the back and climbed into the cab.

Lili wasn't there.

I jumped out and ran around to the passenger side of the truck. There were her tiny footprints through the crust of the snow left over from the last storm, the crushed cereal box and red hearts tossed far and wide. Little birds were feasting on the tiny hearts that were bleeding into the snow.

The man scared her and she hid.

I grabbed the jacket I'd covered her with and shook it, as if she might be hiding inside the folds. I tried to look under the seat, knowing she wasn't that small, there wasn't any space to speak of under there.

I got down on my knees in the snow and looked under the truck; practically crawled underneath so I could see behind every tire. She wasn't there.

Why hadn't she come to me?

My cellphone chimed. Brandy calling. But that couldn't be. There was no service up here. Must be a phenomenon like the hundred-year-old ghosts of dead mules walking and braying or the unburied bodies from centuries past shooting wisps of hell fire and screaming from just under the snow. I can't talk to Brandy until I find Lili.

The light had changed and now I saw wolf tracks in the snow next to her footprints—the impressions of the claws were buried deeper than the backs of the paws and bits of snow thrown up behind, indicating the animal had been running-- fast; after Lili? Now I feared something other had scared her and she ran—but not the man.

Which way? I climbed up onto my truck, onto the load of ties so I could see every which way as far as possible, then something punched me hard in the shoulder. I fell clear down off the load to the ground. I knew what it felt like to be shot. I needed to put some space between Lili and me—and that man—before his shot became truer. Let him have the damn wood.

I still believed he didn't have Lili; I had to find her before he did.

I picked up the cereal box and raked out the beginning of Lili's tracks with the side of my shoes so the man couldn't follow us; then I walked backwards in her steps for as far as I could before the snow grew too heavy to see. Now Nature would complete the cover-up job for me.

I was beginning to feel warm-too warm, it was unnatural, when I stumbled across a solid lump beneath the soft snow. The air turned full-dark and the storm howled at me as I lay across the lump and began digging, brushing the snow away, regretting my earlier self for tossing my gloves into the back of the Jeep. I was searching for a face buried beneath the snow—hoping for an animal if it was dead, or my daughter if she was alive.

My fingers found a face. Human. Child. Cold. Too cold.

I tried to warm her, to bring her back to life until suddenly the child under me stirred. In the dim reflective snow light, I watched, mesmerized as the little girl rose out of the slush and fixed me with bright vacant eyes. She caught me off guard when she reached for me and I hated myself that for a moment I startled and backed away but this was my daughter. I pulled her to me and petted her with tears and soothing words. Then she went wild. She growled and dark spores blew from her mouth. Savage nails dug into neck as viscous blood-spattered teeth snapped at my eyes.

153

I backed away again as I brought my cellphone out and turned on the light. This little frozen girl was not my daughter. Unless the ice crystals had turned her skin whiter, broken off her curls and bloated her with snow. No. Not my daughter. Yet the poor child, someone's daughter, had stepped too far off the path.

The path.

The road!

Highway 138!

I know Lili's not freezing in the snow; I would be able to feel it in the bone marrow that we share. I taught her to go downhill if she was lost in the woods and she'd find water, which would lead her to people.

I'm sorry now, it doesn't seem so smart in this case. If she's not freezing in the snow another danger to my little Lili would be the highway. I'll head down the hill until I reach Highway 138.

Even when I reached the road my phone had no reception. Dark clouds streamed through the black sky. The only illumination was the headlights on the cars that flew by and the gaudy display of lights on the eighteen wheelers that roared past.

There's no room in the sky for the moon to rise. No spot beside the road for a diner or a motel where I could lay my weary head. Besides I don't have time to stare up at the moon or to eat or sleep or even to bleed or die.

That little frozen girl was not my daughter, my daughter is alive somewhere and I'm traveling up and down this highway until I find her if I have to wear the damn road out.

Then out of nowhere, two headlights that weren't obeying the rules came at me, swerving, inescapable, the night around them suddenly darker. I froze like a deer as I stared mesmerized in the glaring randomness of chance. Whack!

I was flat on the side of the road—disassociated—no pain, no vision—just swirls in the blackness. I couldn't move. I listened to my breath in the otherwise silent night. Wheezing. My body steamed. Sensation returned. So warm, finally, warm. One leg shook; I was going to rise. I was not going to stop until I found my child.

I smelled burning rubber then the driver stupidly backed up and almost ran me over. Again?

"I'm sorry, Sir. I'm so sorry." I could smell the cigarette smoke in her hair and the beer on her breath and though her words were mushy I knew right away it was my wife.

"No. Brandy, I'm sorry. I've lost her."

"Jack?" Her body weaved from side to side as she leaned down in the red glow from the taillights. I could tell she was having trouble focusing. "Did I kill you? Are you what dead smells like?" She vomited onto the snow. "Who did you lose?"

She was nothing like my mother; Brandy had no idea that her child was gone and that was more than I could stand.

"Brandy, take this," I slipped my wedding ring into her palm.

I stood up with a purpose greater than my pain and threw my wallet into the snow—I wouldn't need an identity on the road, I'd be traveling too fast for anyone to see or stop me.

I guess I was born lanky for a reason; I stretched out each leg, one after the other, to a legendary length.

I imagine the decades have piled up on me as I've haunted the highways. I've searched for Lili and prayed she's on her own, as I watched for the wolfish man and tasted the wind for his scent. And every time I think of the beast that's hungered after my family my legs get looser and my strides get longer.

Sometimes I cross over to Route 66 and now and then I hike up the Pass and have a gander. My truck's still there, though it's rusted out, nothing but a bare orange skeleton. I circle around for a closer look and once again the irrational spark of hope that begins in my belly turns to ice; no, Lili's not where I left her—sleeping on the seat under my jacket clutching her box of red heart cereal.

That was wishful, magical thinking-I know the road is the answer, not the top of the mountain.

I sigh and hit the longest road again—Route 66 from the Pacific Ocean to Chicago, Illinois—with a vengeful wolf on my trail. He killed my father for stealing the pup and my mother for making the stew that I wouldn't eat: now he wants my daughter, but I'll find her first. I need to find my child.

On Blackened Wings

Michelle Ann King

They'd been driving for at least four hours, maybe five. Dionne's back ached, her bad knee throbbed and her eyes were dried out and burning. Time to get off the road.

The village was one of the empty ones—creepy, but better than the alternatives. Past the clusters of cottages, the tiny post office and dark stone church, she saw a big white building with wide leaded windows, three tall chimneys and a tangle of ivy climbing the brickwork to a sloping thatched roof. A wooden sign at the front called it The Willow Tree Hotel.

She knew the sort of place it must have been, once. Locals on their regular stools at the bar, visitors driving in for rustic, homely food and pints of amber coloured ale beside the fireplace. Music from a jukebox, maybe a live band on weekends. Good days.

Old days.

Dionne drove into the car park and waited for the others to catch up. For a moment it looked like Julian's car wasn't slowing, that he was going to carry on straight past. But at the last minute he turned and screeched through the gate.

Would she have been surprised if he'd decided to drive on? No. Every time they stopped, she expected to find herself alone. Why should they follow her, these people? She'd survived by nothing but chance—just kept driving past the burning wreck that used to be her home. Her town. Kept driving, fighting panic with speed while the skies boiled. She'd picked up other people along the way and every time it happened she expected them to laugh at her, demand to know what the hell gave her the right to make decisions for anyone. She'd waited for it, looked forward to it. She still did.

The rest of their pitifully small convoy filed in behind Julian and parked in a huddled group. Rachel helped her brother out of the van and he lifted his head, scenting the air. To Dionne, it smelled like all these places did—flat and stale. Old. Wrong.

Ben stared into the sky, unblinking. She wondered what he saw, with those clouded eyes. And was grateful that she didn't know.

'They're gone,' he said.

Dionne went around to those still waiting in their cars. 'It's clean,' she said. 'Let's get some sleep and in the morning, we'll stock up.'

Stock up. Such a harmless phrase. As if they were going on a camping trip, instead of looting the possessions of the dead.

The breeze whipped Ben's hair back, exposing the scars. Julian, walking past with Lucas, shielded the boy's eyes. Rachel glared at him until Julian turned away from her, too.

Dionne pulled her jacket closed. The wind was always warm now, but somehow it still made everyone shiver. Like the breath of ghosts.

Ben began to hum softly, an old pop song she recognised but couldn't name. The weight of it, of everything that was gone, sat heavy on her chest. Rock stars and musicals and talent shows, things people did simply because they were fun. Things that had nothing to do with trying to stay alive.

'It's not fair,' she said.

'No, it isn't,' Rachel said, but she was looking at her brother.

'How's he doing?' Dionne asked quietly. She wasn't the worst off, here. It was a fight to remember that, sometimes, but she kept trying.

Rachel shook her head. 'I'm worried about what this is doing to him.' She put her thumb to her mouth, snagged the nail between her teeth. 'They're in his head, Dionne. The bats. Can you imagine, just for a second, what that must be like?'

'No,' Dionne said. She couldn't. Didn't want to.

Bats. The word was inadequate by a dozen orders of magnitude, but there wasn't a better one. Whatever they were—aliens, demons, creatures from some unknown hell—they weren't bats. But maybe it was the closest approximation the mind could stand.

'I'm sorry,' Dionne said. 'I know what he's been through, but we need him.'

Most people didn't survive and they'd all marvelled at how lucky Ben was. At first, anyway.

'What if it wasn't always on him, Dionne? What if we could all take a turn?'

'How could we do that? We're not...' she trailed off, groped for something that would not offend. Failed to find it, and went on, simply, 'Like him.'

159

Rachel didn't respond, just hugged herself and pushed her hair out of her eyes. She seemed more hard-edged, more brittle, than usual. How long since she'd slept?

Rachel watched the others shuffle inside the pub, then said, 'Come on. I'll show you.'

She opened the van's back doors and pulled out a large metal toolbox. She flipped back the lid and, for a second, a humming sound arose, briefly harmonising with Ben.

Inside the box lay a mass of tangled metal and wires, wrapped around something that was twisted and stretched. Something that pulsed, glistening wetly.

Dionne covered her mouth. 'What the hell is that?'

'Last time we stopped, there were some... remains. Parts of bodies, parts of a bat. Ben used them to make this. I don't think I can explain to you how—if I'm honest, I'm not entirely sure I know. But it acts as an external connector—it'll give the rest of us a way to sense them, just like he can.'

Dionne swiped her forearm across her face, where a film of slick sweat had formed. Her stomach was turning over in loose, lazy rolls.

'Put it away,' she said. 'Now.'

Rachel shot her an angry look. 'It's not right to make my brother be the sin eater for us all. We have to help him.'

Dionne held up a hand. 'I know,' she said. 'I know. But—'

'We have to try, Dionne.'

160

Dionne shook her head. Did she believe that Rachel and Ben had built some kind of psychic hotline to the bats, out of wires and roadkill? No. Not for a second.

But if, somehow, they really had—did she want to try it out?

Hell, no.

'I'm sorry,' she said and stumbled away.

***

Inside, the pub was just how she'd imagined—chunky tables and tall stools, a few leather sofas, booths around the sides. Rough painted plaster and a curved bar in polished wood, rows of bottles lined up on mirrored shelves. Chalkboards still listed the restaurant's specials: Grilled trout with almonds, Steak au Poivre. Pecan brownies.

Julian stood behind the bar, a glass of clear liquid in his hand. 'Want a drink?'

The taste in Dionne's mouth was sharp and metallic. She slid onto one of the stools. 'Scotch.'

Julian poured a generous measure. 'What are we doing, Dionne?'

A good question. Or bad, depending on your perspective. 'I don't know,' she said. 'Moving. Keeping going. Staying alive.'

'Is that enough?'

Another bad question. 'It has to be.'

She picked up her glass, watched the tawny liquid roll from side to side. Looked at Julian. A good man, really. Just scared. And they were all scared.

161

'That Ben,' he said, and stopped.

'He's saved our lives, Julian. More than once.'

'Maybe. Maybe we've just been lucky. But he's...' He trailed off, looked away.

'What? Different?'

Julian tapped out an uneven rhythm on the bar's surface. 'I've got Lucas to think of, that's all I'm saying. I've got to look out for my son.'

'I know. But we've all got to look out for each other, now.'

The words, spoken without thinking, tasted as sour as the alcohol. She glanced at the door, but Rachel and Ben didn't come in.

Sin eater. Scapegoat. Sacrifice. Weren't they better than that? Even now, weren't they better?

Yes. They were. They had to be.

She drained her glass, slammed it down and went back out to the car park.

Rachel was still standing by the van, the box at her feet.

'Okay,' Dionne said. 'Let me try it. Quickly, before I change my mind. What do I have to do?'

'It just takes contact. Touch it, that's all.'

Dionne reached inside the box without looking, without stopping to think. Her hands plunged into the tangle of wires and metal. And softer parts.

Fluid, dark and viscous, burned her skin where it dripped. There was a sense of pressure, of something coiling around her wrist. Around her mind. Hollowness in her stomach, lights behind her eyes.

The world inverted, blanked out and reappeared in a riot of colour. Shades and folds, layering and overlapping. Solid and dense, open and empty. A faint buzzing at the edge of her hearing, the sense of a vast hive mind. Alien. Wrong. Beautiful.

She pulled her hands out and stepped back, dizziness threatening to put her down.

Ben put a hand on her arm, steadying her. 'Are you all right?'

'Yes,' she said, and hoped it was true. She tasted ash and smoke, and spat on the concrete. 'That's what it's like, for you? All the time?'

She looked into those flat, opaque eyes and saw understanding. 'Yes,' he said.

'How do you stand it?'

'You learn.'

She shivered, then swayed as her vision greyed and fuzzed.

She woke fully dressed, lying on a bed in a tiny, cramped room with a sloping ceiling. She felt unrested, haunted by dreams—memories?—of dark open spaces and blue fire.

Outside, the others were already waiting. Julian was loading up his car while Lucas kicked a football against the fence. It rebounded and rolled towards Dionne. She kicked it back and Lucas flicked out his foot, bringing it under control. He grinned and she smiled back. Was it hardest for the kids, or easiest?

'There's a garage about half a mile down the road,' Rachel said. 'We should fill up before we leave.'

Julian watched Lucas playing. 'It'll run out, eventually,' he said. 'The petrol. You know that, don't you? We can't keep driving forever.'

163

'We'll work it out,' Dionne said. Hoped she sounded more confident than she felt.

'Will we?'

'Yes,' Ben said. 'We will.' He put his hand on the van's bonnet and it roared into life.

For a long moment, there was no sound other than the rumble of the engine. Lucas tucked his ball under his arm and looked up at Ben.

'That was cool,' he said. 'How did you do that?'

Julian stepped in front of him. 'Go back inside, Lucas.'

'But Dad, I—'

'I said go, Lucas. Now.'

The boy grumbled, but did as he was told.

Julian nodded at the van, still idling. 'Are you going to answer the question? How did you do that, Ben?'

'We have to adapt,' Ben said. 'We have to learn.'

'And what is it you're learning? How to be like them? How to become one of them?'

Dionne raised her hands, palms outward. 'Julian, come on.'

He rounded on her. 'Come on, what? You saw what he just did. Is that normal?'

'What's normal, Julian? What does that word even mean, now?'

Julian shook his head. 'You can't be telling me that you—' He broke off. 'Dionne, what's the matter? What is it?'

'I don't know,' Dionne said. Had she heard something? The choking, ashy taste was back in her throat. She looked at the sky.

Ben echoed her movement, cocking his head. 'They're coming,' he said.

Rachel's hand went to her throat. 'The bats? Now?'

'Yes.'

'Okay, we have to go,' Dionne said. 'Julian, get Lucas. I'll tell the others.'

Julian's face paled, but he didn't move. 'How do we know we can trust him?' He also looked up at the sky, empty and quiet. 'He could be leading us straight to them.'

Rachel curled her lip. 'You're an idiot,' she said and threw her bags in the back of the van. 'We're getting out of here before they come. You can do what you want.'

Dionne put her hand on Julian's arm. 'It's true,' she said. 'They're coming. If you don't trust Ben, then trust me. Get your boy. We have to go, right now.'

She left him, ran without looking back. Reached the pub, threw the doors wide and screamed out the alarm. Hammered on doors, yelled out a rollcall of names. Held down panic by force of will. By necessity.

People fled their rooms, eyes glazed but movements quick and efficient—the desperate resignation of a familiar nightmare.

The evacuation was complete in under five minutes, car doors slammed and engines running. Hot, metallic-tasting air leaked through the windows as Dionne drove and the sky darkened to a sepia brown. The colour of old blood.

In the rear-view mirror, the Willow Tree began to crumble. The chimney wavered and toppled, shattering into rubble. The roof slid down, a slow motion avalanche of slate and dust. In total, eerie silence, the building melted into ruin.

The air sharpened, smelled like ozone. Through the ringing in Dionne's ears, a resonant, shrieking cry. Another. A hundred. A thousand.

Dionne slammed her foot on the accelerator and the van lurched forward. The numbers on the dashboard clock ticked over in a dizzying blur. A huge oak tree at the side of the road blackened and died, fell slowly and silently backwards. Dionne screamed, her head full of wings.

The harsh blare of a horn penetrated the noise and Rachel's van pulled in front of her. Dionne focused on its lights, kept her foot down and followed it through the churning air.

The road disappeared at some point, but the ground stayed firm under her wheels. They drove through fog that gleamed with a yellowish light, straight through diseased-looking trees and mossy walls that melted away like ghosts.

Dionne's arms shook and her eyes stung, but she kept driving. Kept following Rachel. Following Ben.

After a while—it could have been minutes, it could have been years—the world outside solidified and settled. Became urban. A recognisable landscape, if a broken one.

Many of the roads they came across were impassable, but they managed to manoeuvre into a residential street lined with tall, four-storey houses that looked mostly intact. Dionne stopped the van, got out and sat on the kerb. She put her head between her knees until the pounding in her temples slowed down and the nausea receded.

Julian helped Lucas out of the car. 'Are we safe here?' he asked.

Dionne was too exhausted to tell if it was concern or sarcasm in his voice. 'I don't know,' she said. 'I don't even know what that word means anymore.'

'We will be,' Ben said. He had his arm around his sister, who looked pale and sick.

'Is everyone okay?' she said.

'I think so,' Dionne said. 'How about you? How do you feel?'

'Drained. My head hurts. Business as usual, really.' She gave them a weak smile.

Dionne helped them carry the bags inside the nearest house. The furnishings looked expensive but old fashioned—dressers and writing desks and a giant claw-footed bath tub. Mottled wallpaper and grey, swirling oil paintings of storms and warships. Stains that could have been memories of mould, or rust. Or blood.

Claustrophobia quickly drove her outside again. Already, darkness was falling. It seemed as if the nights were twice as long as the days, now. Sunlight was something from a dream.

Julian was leaning against his car, a cigarette clamped between two fingers.

'I didn't know you smoked,' she said.

'I don't,' he said. 'I gave up a long time ago. When Lucas was born.' He held the cigarette up in front of his eyes, turning it from one side to the other. 'But it hardly seems to matter now, does it? I don't think it's going to be lung cancer that kills us.'

'You shouldn't talk like that,' Dionne said. But she took the cigarette when he offered it and inhaled deeply.

'I'm sorry,' he said. 'For the way I am, sometimes. I ought to be thanking you, I know you're doing your best. Everyone is, I know that. Even—' he jerked his head at the house behind her. 'Him. Even if he does scare me shitless.'

He took another drag on the cigarette. 'It's Lucas, that's the thing. I worry about Lucas all the time. I worry about how I'm going to look after him, when I don't understand what's happened to us, or how the world works, now. I don't understand anything, any more. We're just scrabbling around in the dark here. What are we supposed to do, Dionne? What are we supposed to do?'

Without waiting for an answer, he dropped the cigarette on the floor, trod on it and went back inside.

Dionne watched the sky. Heavy clouds obscured the moon, but there was no rain. She couldn't remember the last time there had been rain.

She opened the back door of Rachel's van, got in and closed the door behind her. The toolbox sat on a pile of rags, pushed up against the side. She sat back on her heels and looked at it.

What do you do, when you don't understand?
You learn.

Dionne flipped open the lid and reached inside.
Something fluttered against her hand and the
familiar sick churning hit hard. The inside of the
van lit up, agonisingly bright. She screwed her eyes
shut, but the blaze refused to dim. The metal walls
fell away, became transparent. The houses beyond
were just as ghostly, walls thin and insubstantial.
Wavering lines and incorporeal shapes.

And beyond them, that constant, rolling wave
of noise. A vast presence, fractured but coherent. A
whole greater than the sum of its parts.

Hot tears scalded her cheeks and sounds
brushed at the back of her mind, a symphony of
whispers from things that had no voices. She fought
the way they burned, and listened.

Listened, heard. Understood.

Dionne opened her eyes, wrenched her hands
out of the box and scrambled from the van. She fell
into the road, scraping and grazing her skin, but felt
nothing. Her head was still buzzing.

She got to her feet and ran for the house.
Rachel was asleep on the sofa, Ben standing by the
window.

'There are bats here,' she said.

He didn't turn round. 'Yes.'

'You knew. You knew, and yet you brought us
here.' She grabbed his shoulder, made him face her.
'You said it was clean, Ben.'

'No. I said we'd be safe.'

'Is there supposed to be a difference?'

'Yes,' he said.

169

Rachel stirred, lifted herself up. 'Dionne? What's happening?'

'Bats. Here.'

Rachel shot into wakefulness, sitting up and swinging her legs onto the floor. 'Oh, God. Then we have to go.'

Dionne reached out to help her stand. 'Yes.'

'No,' said Ben.

Dionne whirled on him. 'I told the others they were wrong, Ben. They're scared of you, they don't trust you, but I defended you. I swore you were on our side. But you brought us right to where they are. Why would you do that? Why?'

Rachel looked up at her brother, frowning. 'Ben?'

'Because they're everywhere,' he said. He looked at Dionne. 'You understand that now, don't you? You felt them. Julian was right, back at the village. We can't keep running. There's nowhere left to run to.'

Dionne curled her hands into fists. 'Then what? What do you want us to do, Ben? Give up?'

'No. Fight.'

Dionne laughed, and had to work hard to stop it spiralling away from her into hysteria. 'How the hell are we supposed to do that?'

Ben stepped forward and grabbed both her wrists. Where their skin touched, light flared. He raised her hands in his and blue flame rose up from them. 'You know how,' he said.

The silence spun out, gained a power of its own. Then Rachel said, 'For God's sake, you're

170

going to set the place on fire,' and the moment was broken.

Dionne pulled away and they stamped out the smouldering patches on the floor.

'So,' Rachel said, when the fire was out. 'Would anyone like to explain what just happened?'

'I wish I could,' Dionne said, staring at her hands. They were unmarked.

'They're strong because they're together,' Ben said. 'We can be, too.'

Rachel stared at him. It was an expression Dionne had seen many times on the others' faces, but never on Rachel's. She watched the girl fight it. 'What are you talking about?'

'What we made is more than just a window,' he said. 'It's a conduit. It means we can do more than just find them—we can join with them.'

'And why in God's name would we want to do that?'

Ben knelt down beside his sister and took her hand. Dionne saw the effort it took Rachel not to flinch.

'Don't you understand?' he said. 'This is our chance.'

'To do what, Ben?'

'How many times have you said that things have changed? This is their world, now. If we still want to live in it, then we have to change too. All of us.'

A loud, protracted shriek ripped through the air, and for a long moment Dionne didn't understand that it wasn't just in her head. Then Julian appeared in the doorway, his eyes wild.

171

'Bats,' he screamed.

'Come on,' Ben said, and ran outside. Rachel shot Dionne a terrified look, but followed.

A hot, rank wave of air rolled over them. Rachel gagged and stumbled, but Ben pushed her towards the van. 'Get in,' he said. 'Quickly.'

The shrieking began to break up, lose its cohesion. It became higher, more discordant. Julian grabbed Lucas and threw him on the ground, covering the boy with his own body. Dionne's ears were ringing, her sense of direction gone—but then she realised the sound was coming not from overhead but from ground level. From close by.

Ben stood in the middle of the road, his head thrown back and his mouth open wide. The shriek of the bats ripped out from his throat and spiralled upwards.

He looked at Dionne and said, 'Help me.' Not in words, not out loud. But she heard.

She struggled to his side and grabbed his hand. Opened her mind and her throat. Lent her voice to his.

Then Rachel was with them, on her knees, one hand plunged inside the metal box and the other reaching out. Dionne seized her wrist, held on tight.

Rachel screamed, a human sound that gradually thinned, became harsher. Her eyes darkened and her mouth stretched wide.

Somewhere behind them Julian's voice formed a counterpoint, stumbling and hitching but repetitive, a rhythm Dionne eventually recognised as prayer.

Above, the black air exploded into flame. The bats' blue fire, which she'd seen scorch the earth so many times, now raked across the sky. Their shriek was answered, doubled, tripled, fractured into a thousand dissonant echoes. The ground shook under her feet, as if trying to tear itself apart.

Then it was over and there was only silence and Dionne cried out with the shock of it. The sudden absence was like vertigo, like falling, like the end of the world. Her vision was strobing, flashes of black and blue. Fire fell like rain and she curled into a ball and put her hands over her head. Cried like a child.

A hand slid under her arm, helped her to her feet. Rachel.

'They're gone,' she said. 'It's over.'

Dionne's knees buckled, but Rachel caught her and kept her upright. She looked around, saw the same shell-shocked expression on a lot of faces.

Julian was still crushing Lucas to his body, although the boy was doing his best to squirm free. 'What did you do?' Julian said. 'What the hell did you just do?'

Rachel answered. The inside of her mouth was black. 'We didn't run,' she said.

Lucas finally struggled out of Julian's grip and ran to Dionne. 'Your eyes,' he said, reaching up to her. 'Can you still see?'

She squatted in front of him and let him touch her face. 'Oh, yes,' she said. 'I can see. I can see so much.'

Julian stared into the sky, his head whipping around in all directions. 'Are they gone?'

173

'For now,' Ben said. 'And when there are enough of us, for good. They have enough territory of their own. They won't fight for this.'

'So are we going to stay here?' Lucas said. 'Is this where we live, now?' He craned his head back around to look at Julian. 'Dad? Can I have my football?'

Julian said nothing. Dionne followed his gaze to the front garden of the house behind them. There was a dark shape under the hedge, the suggestion of a twisted wing.

Ben and Rachel, holding hands, crouched beside her. Rachel leant against her back, skin warm through the thin material of Dionne's shirt.

Dionne leaned forward and slid her hand under the hedge. The dark shape flared blue and crumbled into ash.

All three straightened up, and Dionne smiled at Lucas. 'Yes,' she said. 'This is where we live now.'

Ice Crystals

Travis Mushanski

"Uncle Scott?"

Scott sighed. He had now heard the boy call out to him one hundred times. The falling snow dropped the highway visibility to nearly zero and, to make matters worse, the sun had just dipped below the horizon.

"Call me Dad," he explained, prying his hand off the steering wheel to pat the boy's thigh. "Okay, Jacey?"

Jacey squirmed against a pillow propped against the passenger door. The shoulder strap of his seat belt, being too large for his five-year-old frame, had been tucked behind his back. "Uncle…I mean, Dad?" The boy corrected his speech, nervously fingering his stuffed bear.

"I miss my mom," he murmured, a touch louder than a whisper. He sniffled and rubbed his eyes.

"I know, buddy." Scott switched on the truck's high beams, but quickly shut them off: he could only see a wall of falling snow. He wiggled to the edge of the driver's seat and squinted into the growing gloom of the Saskatchewan highway.

"But like I told you, this is a boy's trip." He blindly ran a hand through the boy's hair, playing with his shoulder length braid. "Besides, your mom just has to do a bit of work around the house and she's going to meet us at the hotel. Two days, tops!"

Jacey released an exasperated sigh. "I've never been to a hotel," he declared through a long yawn. "Is it going to be fun?"

"Ya, buddy. We can go swimming and they have a waters—"

"Scott, look out!" Jacey shouted, his finger jutted towards the blizzard.

Time slowed to a painful crawl. A massive brown shape stood rooted in the highway: its eyes floating discs of yellow and steam bellowing from its nostrils. Scott slammed on the brakes, sending the truck skidding sideways on a sheet of black ice. He cursed and yanked the steering wheel away from the snow-filled ditch. The tires bit into the asphalt, seconds before plowing into the darkness.

"Jesus fuckin' Christ!" He swore at the animal, narrowly missing the steadfast creature. Its jet-black eyes watched the skidding motor vehicle with curiosity.

Scott slowed the vehicle and ran a hand through his receding hair. His heart felt like a brick in his chest and his lungs constricted, causing his breathing to go ragged. He snatched his beer out of the cup holder and guzzled the last third of its contents.

"It was an elk!" Jacey was on his knees, searching out the window for another.

"Ain't no elk around here," Scott grumbled. "Just a deer, is all."

"Mom said the elk is part of all of us. It's those that came before. Our family calls it Wapiti. It protects us and gives us strength."

Scott blew a raspberry and chuckled. "I think it's time for little boys to go to sleep," he said in a stern voice. *Enough of this Indian bullshit.*

Scott's head jolted up. Panic stretched open his heavy-lidded eyes. His heart raced with sudden terror at the sound of the tires grinding over the road's rumble strips. Endorphins flooded his system, causing his mouth to run dry. He had fallen asleep at the wheel and his arms quivered to regain control of the speeding truck.

The wind howled, blowing heavy snow across the Saskatchewan highway. Only the mounds of ice, left behind from graders clearing last week's snowfall, marked the edges of the road. At some point he'd left behind the coniferous forests of the Prince Albert area and had moved into the province's barren prairies.

Scott leaned over the steering wheel, unable to see past the blizzard cocooning the vehicle. He shook his head and stroked his graying goatee. *Gotta be close to Saskatoon now,* he thought. *Wait out the storm and b-line it straight south on the number 11. Be in the States in no time.*

Scott fiddled with the radio knob, trying to block out the road noise, but could only find static. Its low hum was hypnotic, soothing almost, but threatened to send him back into the dream world. He slapped an arrhythmic beat on his dash and watched the radio tuner race through each station with little success.

" . . . *breaking news from the CBC news desk. The RCMP is asking everyone to stay off of all*

177

Saskatchewan highways for the foreseeable future. An Alberta clipper is wreaking havoc across the province at this hour with heavy winds and heavy snowfall. Visibility is next to zero, leaving travellers stranded . . ."

"No fricken kidding, CBC," Scott chuckled. The radio station scratched in and out of existence. He scrounged behind his seat for any undrunk beers, but came up empty handed.

" . . . RCMP are also on the look out for a blue F150 Ford Pickup. Licence plate number HYP 598. Driver is male. Age is mid-to-late thirties. He is considered dangerous but unarmed. He is believed to be travelling with a young boy from Wahpeton Dakota Nation, who has recently been reported missing—"

"Ahh, shit," Scott cursed, pawing at the radio until it turned off. Jacey stirred and groaned in the passenger seat.

A gust of wind pushed the F150 into the center of the highway and Scott had to yank on the steering wheel to keep the vehicle on the road. The blizzard spiraled around him in a never-ending tunnel of blowing snow. The headlights made the snow shimmer like walls of ice and the vehicle steered straight into a void of blackness at the end of it.

Yellow eyes blazed to life in the corner of his peripheral. He twisted to see the twirling eyes that hovered next to Jacey's window, but they slunk into the rear of the vehicle and faded into the darkness. Scott caught a fleeting image in the rear-view mirror: a shadow pranced across the pitch-black highway.

Something struck the driver side headlight with a heavy thud. The vehicle shuddered and Scott growled through gritted teeth. His hands strangled the steering wheel, knuckles white in desperation. A tap on his side window drew his attention to the steaming face of a mule deer, slotting in pace with the truck. Scott screamed and hammered the gas pedal to the floor, but the deer casually ran across the truck's path into the darkness.

"Fuck was that," Scott called out into the blizzard. Shivers broke out across his body and he started to hyperventilate. *A crash out here would mean certain death.* He glanced down at the boy who quietly snored: he was dead to the world.

A blinding light bloomed around the speeding truck, forcing Scott to squint. Dozens, maybe hundreds, of golden eyes lit either side of the snow tunnel. Deer leapt from side to side, dashing through the snow like splashing dolphins. The truck jerked amongst a herd of deer jostling for control of the vehicle.

Scott's scream reverberated across the tunnel of snow and in union, the deer dove upwards to be swept away by the storm. Their bodies burst into snowflakes, but to Scott's horror, they weaved themselves together into the form of a great elk.

It stood motionless in the void of blackness, a static image, neither shrinking nor growing, while the truck sped towards it. The great beast tilted back its head and released a blood curdling chuckle. In that instant, the snow melted from its body, revealing a gleaming coat of tan fur. On top of its muscular neck sat a skeleton head with a massive rack of antlers, blazing with blue flames.

The truck ploughed through the great beast, smearing its existence through space and time. Each contorted phase of the elk's death hung frozen like a polaroid snapshot. They stretched outward behind the F150 to form a grotesque elk centipede. The truck itself came to a sudden stop, quivering at the end of a cosmic elastic band.

Scott howled at the truck's sudden reversal, sending him soaring backwards through the frozen images of the dead elk. He crashed through each gore filled frame until the creature reformed itself from the shards of its past selves.

Time returned to normal and Scott found himself plunging through the icy snow tunnel towards the reborn Elk. *No, not Elk,* he thought. *Wapiti.* He stomped on the brake, but the truck no longer responded to his commands. The steering and acceleration were hell bent on colliding with the creature.

The beast twisted, narrowly avoiding impact with the truck. It twisted fiery antlers and struck the F150, sheering off the cab's roof in one vicious slash. Bitterly cold ice bit into Scott's exposed skin. He tried to cover his face with his flannel jacket, but frostbite quickly spread across his flesh.

Scott opened his eyes in time to see the Wapiti charging headfirst at the truck. Ice crystals flooded into his lungs and froze his screams into blocks of ice. The momentum of the elk's strike sent the vehicle tumbling head over tails through the night sky. Metal carnage rained down across the Canadian prairies.

***

Constable Rakoff stood on the edge of the highway, staring in shock at the destruction caused by one vehicle. Remains of the F150 were scattered across more than five hundred feet of ice and snow. Whatever made the truck lose control, caused it to roll that entire distance, shedding metal, plastic and glass along its way?

"Like we said, officer," the aboriginal man said, interrupting Rakoff's stoic gaze. "We saw the smoke when we drove by. The storm had subsided, but it's still quite cold."

"So, we thought we should make sure everyone was alright," the woman broke into the conversation. Rakoff assumed it was the old man's wife.

"Are you sure you don't want to do this in the cruiser?" The bitterly cold morning had started to gnaw its way through his winter layers.

"Our people live for this type of weather," he smiled and playfully slapped Rakoff on the shoulder. He wore only a Prince Albert Raiders ball cap, fur lined suede jacket and a pair of worn blue jeans. "Besides, we wanted to show you where we found the boy."

The old man led Rakoff up the road to a path of footprints that meandered into a farmer's field. They seemed to be approaching a large piece of

181

debris, part of the truck bed attached to the rear axle, but suddenly veered into the open field.

"How did you manage to—"

"The steam from the deer's collected bodies acted as a beacon," the woman explained. She pulled her beanie toque down over her exposed ears and hugged herself to stay warm.

"Deer?" Rakoff asked, stepping into a clearing free of snow.

"Yes. Deer," the elderly man said. He spun, arms wide open, in the center of the clearing. He knelt to pluck a handful of grass. He smelled it and nodded his head with certainty. "Many of them. Maybe four, or five."

The woman wrapped her arm around Rakoff's and smiled up at him. "They kept him warm. Kept him safe."

"You look confused, son," the man said. He patted Rakoff's shoulder again, acting like the grandfather Rakoff never knew. The old man latched onto his other arm and, with his wife's assistance, they led him to the center of the clearing.

"Okay, now. I don't know what this is all about but—"

The woman shushed Rakoff and the old man said, "Look. Feel. You must believe."

Rakoff allowed the couple to pull him to his knees and place his hand onto the earth of the clearing. To his astonishment, the ground still retained heat.

"But, how?" He asked the simple question, knowing there would be no simple answers. He knew the boy was safe and sound in the back of his

182

cruiser. He had checked him over and he didn't find a hair out of place. How did the boy survive such a horrific crash?

An answer came in the form of a high pitched bugle call, fluttering amongst the icy breeze. He scrambled to his feet in time to see a great elk galloping into the distance. It moved into the horizon and faded into a fog of shimmering ice. It had returned to the white wilderness from whence it came. The sound of hooves gliding atop crystalized snowbanks echoed across the frozen prairies.

"Constable?"

The feminine voice pulled Rakoff back to reality and he realised he stood alone in a farmer's field. He blinked the snow from his eyes and spun around. The red and blue lights of the emergency vehicles destroyed the picturesque illusion he had been drawn into. He wiped the icicles off his mustache and stepped out of the clearing towards the woman in uniform.

"Ya, sorry. Alisha, right? Just a little bit over my head out here," he explained, flashing the woman an awkward smile.

"Understandable," she acknowledged, gesturing to the smoldering wreckage. "Listen, Constable," she sighed, readying to reveal the bad news. "we still got some ground to cover, but there's no sign of the perp."

"Didn't imagine there would be," he muttered under his frosty breath. Ice crystals caught the sunlight at the perfect angle, marking the beauty of the prairies with a golden aura.

"Pardon me?" Alisha asked, tilting her head.

"Come on. The dead can wait," he called over his shoulder. "There's a mother out there who's worried sick and I'm sure she would love to know her son is safe."

Highways

Paul Edwards

I met Lucy in *The Cellar* - a dark, cavernous bar under Welch Road. As our eyes locked from across the room, I was blown away by her beauty. Her thin, almost porcelain face was perfectly framed by long black hair. She wore a grey Nirvana "Smiley" T-shirt and ripped denim jeans.

It took all my courage to approach her, but I needn't have worried; Lucy was warm, open, funny. Turned out we'd both attended the same primary school. We also shared an enthusiasm for Nick Cave records and Elmore Leonard novels.

"So," she picked a strand of hair away from her eyes, "what do you do?".

"I'm a wound care specialist for a medical company," I replied. "Nothing exciting. You?"

Lucy was a hairdresser. She owned a salon in Alverstoke Village and was doing extremely well for herself. "It's all starting to come together, you know? Like I've finally found my place in the world."

We talked for over an hour, perched together on a hard bench in an alcove at the back of the bar. Posters for clubs and rock bands plastered the brick walls around us. It felt like our own dark cosmos: we were so utterly, so perfectly alone there.

At the end of the evening, I peeled the label off a beer bottle and scribbled my number on the back of it. "Here," I said, passing it to her. "I'd really like to do this again sometime."

A smile spilled across her face.

It made me feel like we were the only two people in the world.

In the market along High Street, I bought a glass-framed picture of Route 101. This was on the same day that Lucy moved in with me. Route 101 is now, of course, the famous Hollywood Freeway. It's the road where Norma Jean Baker posed for one of her first photo shoots shortly before her reincarnation as Marilyn Monroe. I've always been obsessed with long, dusty desert highways. I dream of driving from Los Angeles into the Nevada Desert in one of those old convertible Cadillacs. It's a faded postcard dream I know, but I like to look at it once in a while.

I took the picture back to my apartment and hung it over our bed. Like the view of the sea through my window, it reminded me that nobody's ever really tied to anything.

"I want to travel," I told Lucy as I hammered a nail in the wall. "I don't want to stay in this depressing corner of England my whole life."

Lucy moved toward the window, seeming sullen, gazing out at the black waves crashing and disintegrating around the Isle of Wight.

"But I've got everything I want here," she said. "My shop, my family. I couldn't even imagine leaving."

A year passed. Lucy's business was going great guns; to cope with the demand, she had to employ a couple of students from St. Vincent's College. But

I'd grown bored with my own job. I was anxious to do something else, to escape the nine-to-five day. Lucy knew I wanted to move from Gosport, and it put a serious strain on our relationship.

One afternoon, it came to a head.

"It feels like we're pulling in opposite directions," she said, a note of desperation in her voice. "I'm going to stay at Mum's for a while, Dan. I think we both need some space; some time alone."

I watched her speed off in her Fiesta, then let the front room curtain flap back into place.

I decided to take a walk outside, to get some air, to try and clear my mind of clutter. It was bitter cold out, snow swirling down from the sky to settle on the pavements and roads. I ended up by Alver creek. Dilapidated fishing boats sliced out of the mire. As my eyes roamed the mud, litter and debris, I saw something odd - something *impossible* - under Alver Bridge.

I scaled the railings, dropping down into the darkness of the embankment. I trudged through thick mud, wastepaper blowing about my ankles. I ducked beneath the bridge, tilting my head to one side as I studied it.

The hole was about six inches in length, maybe an inch or two wide. I pushed my finger into it, making it real. My finger lost all sensation, turning cold and dead. I drew it out quickly, shivered, then turned away, hurrying out from under the bridge toward the normality of the town centre.

Night was falling by the time I arrived home. My apartment accreted darkness in layers, like earth heaped onto a grave.

187

Just before ten, the telephone rang.

"We need to talk."

Lucy.

"Yeah. I know."

"Pick me up from work tomorrow. Don't be late."

I put the phone down, and there was a power cut. Everything went – lights, TV, clock. It only lasted a few seconds. But the silence, coupled with the claustrophobic darkness, felt terrifying.

***

Lucy worked quickly as snow pattered against the window, nattering away to the woman in the chair about last night's episode of *Friends*.

I felt a twinge of irritation.

After her last customer left, Lucy locked up the salon and I drove us home. Streetlights cast our white faces onto the darkness of the windscreen.

"Human nature fascinates me," she said, having sensed my irritation back at the shop. "I want to know about people, Dan. Is that so bad?"

Back home, the apartment felt colder than usual. I closed the door, kicked off my shoes. Lucy switched on the TV.

"I thought we were going to talk," I said.

"Too tired. Let's leave it until tomorrow."

I drifted over to the window, planting the flats of my hands against the glass. "I'm going for a walk then," I replied.

Outside, the snow had stopped. A brittle slice of moon emitted a cold light, fluorescently harsh, guiding me toward the creek. I kept telling myself that what I had seen the other day hadn't been real.

The river reeked of tar, salt, and mud. I glanced up and down the street, then carefully scaled the railings.

Despite the night you could still see it.

I wrapped my coat around me, trying to make sense of it all over again.

"What does it mean?"

I wheeled.

A teenager was stood on the bank, next to a discarded fridge. His face was drenched in cold, cold moonlight.

"I don't know," I whispered, turning to it again.

That was when I noticed the crowd, congregating on the towpath above, staring down at the bridge with eyes as black and empty as the hole.

***

The next day there was a quiet, almost subdued air to the office. I surfed the Internet and looked at websites on travel and tourism, just to relieve the boredom. I gazed at pictures of Highway 101 and the US 50 before downloading a Route 66 screensaver.

In the afternoon, I had to train up a new girl called Claire. She sat with me as I showed her how to use our computer system. She talked. I didn't.

"I've just finished a three-year Economics degree at Southampton University," she told me as we waited for the computer to warm up. "It's weird how your life can change at the drop of a hat. I dumped my boyfriend on the day of my graduation. We'd been going out together for four years – well, on and off, anyway. Now, I feel great. It's good to be free of him. God, does that sound callous?"

I shrugged, shaking my head.

"Now I know who I am, and what I can achieve with my life. The world's exciting again, like it is when you're a child."

She laughed.

Whenever the light fell into her eyes, it was like somebody dropping a stone into a pool. Highways formed and reformed; roads more exotic and dangerous than any I'd seen before.

Later, she said: "I moved from Southampton to start afresh. I don't know this area at all. Perhaps you could show me around? I'd like to know where the best clubs and bars are."

She smiled at me from behind her hair. I wondered how much she meant by that.

I was home by six. As I snapped the kitchen light on, I saw the note from Lucy tacked to the refrigerator. *Staying at Mum's tonight. See you soon. L.*

***

"You should stop trying to cling to one another," Darren said, leaning back in his chair. "It's obviously doing more harm than good."

Darren was a mate of mine – we'd worked together in the dockyards a few years back. We were at his favourite haunt, *Nelson's*, a dingy pub located on the corner of High Street.

190

"We're at that stage where we're too frightened to cement what we've got," I said, "and too afraid to break up. It's like we're stuck in some kind of vacuum."

I remembered something Lucy had once said – *"Even if we'd been born at opposite ends of the Earth, we'd still have found each other. Our roads would have crossed somehow."*

Darren's eyes were bloodshot. "You okay?" I asked, leaning across the table.

He shrugged. "I'm not sleeping. But it's no different for anyone else. People are retreating, hiding inside themselves. And it's not just because of this weather."

I glanced across at the window. High Street was deserted. Litter and dead leaves flapped against the steps of the old Methodist church.

"Weird how quiet everything is," I whispered.

Darren wasn't listening. He was huddled over the table, staring into his pint.

I left my seat and walked over to the bar. As I searched my pockets for change, a crowd of people passed by the window. Their voices seemed to bring the night alive. Darren stood up suddenly, knocking his chair to the floor. "Come on," he said, shrugging into his coat. "If we're quick enough, we can catch them."

It had started snowing again. Flakes dusted the roads, moonlight drenched the terraces. At the base of each house was its own crooked shadow.

We followed the crowd through a maze of streets. There were more people near the river, standing around in gangs, or sitting beside small makeshift fires. Most had found a space on the bank or under the bridge itself, but there were also figures loitering on the road above, their outlines sketched out by the streetlights.

"Must be hundreds of us," I breathed.

Darren wasn't listening. He jolted into life, clambered quickly over the railings, dropping like a stone into darkness. From under the bridge, people began to raise their voices in song. Candle flames flickered in the darkness like tongues.

An elderly man at my elbow said: "It's bigger now. It's getting bigger all the time. Reckon soon they'll be able to fit a person through it. And then what?"

***

I woke the next morning with a start, blinking, groaning, tossing back the covers and heading straight for the window. I pulled back the curtain and gazed in utter disbelief at the world outside.

I anxiously touched the window, hoping and praying it was just the glass that was cracked and not the sky.

I sat down on the edge of the bed, gripping my knees, wondering if it was worth going to work. Oddly, I thought of Claire. I wondered if she would be in today.

Even if we'd been born at opposite ends of the Earth, we'd still have found each other.

I left my apartment and wandered the streets, unnerved by the dereliction and silence. The remains of snow salted car windscreens and rooftops. I walked along a deserted Welch Road, then took the iron staircase down to *The Cellar*. The bar seemed even darker than usual.

I walked over to an alcove, and a pale face peeled itself from the darkness.

"Funny how well we know each other." Lucy scraped a strand of hair away from her eyes. She was sat on our bench, sipping a large glass of red wine.

I took my coat off and folded it over the back of a chair. I wanted to ask her why she wasn't with everybody else. Instead, I asked: "Has it really been two and a half years since we first met here? I remembered thinking, *there's nowhere else I want to be*."

I reached out and touched her face. "Why doesn't anybody *talk* about it?" she whispered, smoothing the rim of her glass.

"Do you want another drink?"

"No. Thanks. But help yourself, Dan, there's no one here. Take whatever you want."

I sidled behind the bar, grabbed a tumbler and helped myself to the scotch. "We did see it," she called out. "I mean, we're not going to fool each other over that, right? Because there's no point in *not* talking about it."

I glanced at her. She reached out across the table for her cigarettes, her pretty dark eyes not leaving my face.

"They've found other tears, holes, whatever you want to call them. In London, in Manchester. Places abroad. They're turning up *everywhere*. There's a large tear in Giza, near the Pyramids. People are flocking to them in their thousands." Her voice trembled. "Did you *see* the sky this morning?"

"Yes," I said.

"What's going on out there, Dan?"

I sat down next to her. Lucy put her head on my shoulder. "Everyone's going or gone," she whispered. "There's no one."

Beyond our alcove, beyond our cosmos, the darkness thickened. I couldn't tell whether it was the dark or just... nothingness.

"I'm here," I said, after a pause. "I'm beside you. Even if there's no one else, it doesn't matter."

I pulled her close to me and felt her tears on my skin, so warm and silent.

Then we held each other for what seemed like forever, too afraid to let go.

Meet the Authors

Edward Ahern resumed writing after forty odd years in foreign intelligence and international sales. He's had over three hundred stories and poems published so far, and six books. Ed works the other side of writing at Bewildering Stories, where he sits on the review board and manages a posse of six review editors.

> https://www.twitter.com/bottomstripper
> https://www.facebook.com/EdAhern73/?ref=bookmarks
> https://www.instagram.com/edwardahern1860/

Olivia Arieti lives in Torre del Lago Puccini, Italy, with her family. She writes drama, poetry and fiction. Her stories have appeared in several magazines and anthologies including, *Enchanted Conversations, Enchanted Tales Literary Magazine, Fantasia Divinity Magazine, Forgotten Tomb Press, Horrified Press, Infective Ink, Pandemonium Press, Sirens Call Publications, Blood Song Books, Black Hare Press, Pussy Magic Magazine, Stormy Island Publishing, Breaking Rules Publishing, Scarlet Leaf Review, Iron Faerie Publishing, Dark Dossier Magazine, Paramour Ink Press, Raven and Drake Publishing.*

Dorothy Davies is an editor, writer, photographer and medium. Somehow all these things come together in her seemingly crowded leisure and work life. She retired from editing for a while to run a second hand shop, the best one on the Isle of Wight, but the thrill of finding and publishing outstanding stories became too much so she started again with the Gravestone Press imprint. She still runs the shop…Her book, The Skullface Chronicles, the story of a zombie taking revenge on his dysfunctional family, is available through fiction4all.com. She has a store of short stories, some of which are finding their way into the anthologies, having not seen daylight for many a long year. She also channels books from spirit authors, notable figures from our history. These can be found on the fiction4all.site under Zadkiel Publishing.

Stuart Holland is the owner of Fiction4All, a golf enthusiast (especially the 19th hole) and has written in the genres of crime/mystery, thrillers and suspense and has now turned his hand to horror. His books are available from fiction4all.com in both digital and print editions. His other interests include conspiracy theories, the Knights Templars and has a fascination for the paranormal and supernatural. Which may explain why he wrote 2020-Wipeout a couple of years before Covid-19 had ever been mentioned!

Carl Hughes is a writer and journalist who has worked for the national and provincial press in the UK and has had his articles published worldwide, from the UK to Australia, India to the US. His fiction has appeared in many anthologies and magazines and he has won numerous writing competitions. He specialises in writing about the offbeat and bizarre, with a special love of horror and *Twilight Zone*-type stories. He is married and lives in Norfolk with wife Linda.

Rickey Rivers Jr was born and raised in Alabama. He is a Best of the Net nominated writer and cancer survivor. His work has appeared in the JJ Outre Review, Stellium Literary Magazine, Fabula Argentea (among other publications).

Rie Sheridan Rose multitasks. A lot. Her short stories appear in numerous anthologies, including Killing It Softly Vol. 1 & 2, Hides the Dark Tower, Dark Divinations and On Fire. She has authored twelve novels, six poetry chapbooks and lyrics for dozens of songs. She is also editor-in-chief for Mocha Memoirs Press and editor for the Thirteen O' Clock imprint of Horrified Press. She tweets as @RieSheridanRose.

SJ Townend hopes that her stories take the reader on a journey to often a dark place and only sometimes back again.

SJ won the Secret Attic short story contest (Spring 2020), has had fiction published with Sledgehammer Lit Mag, Hash Journal, Ghost Orchid Press, Bandit Fiction, Black Hare Press, Black Petals Horror Magazine, Ellipsis Zine, Gravely Unusual, Gravestone Press, Holy

Flea, Horla Horror and was long listed for the Women on Writing non-fiction contest in 2020.

She has also written and self-published two dark mystery novels, both of which are available to purchase on Amazon: (Tabitha Fox Never Knocks, Twenty-Seven and the Unkindness of Crows).

Follow her on Twitter: @SJTownend

David Turnbull is a member of the Clockhouse London group of genre writers. He writes mainly short fiction and has had numerous short stories published in magazines and anthologies. His stories have previously been featured at Liars League London events and read at other live events such as Solstice Shorts and Virtual Futures. He was born in Scotland, but now lives in the Catford area of London. He can be found at www.tumsh.co.uk.

Dona Fox writes short stories and poetry, mainly horror and dark mysteries infused with bits of science fiction. Coming from the Pacific edge of the United States, specters from the Northwest's rainforests, Portland's bridges & Seattle's mean streets often creep into her dark tales.

Michelle Ann King is a short story writer from Essex, England. Her stories of fantasy, science fiction, crime, and horror have appeared in over a hundred different venues, including Strange Horizons, Interzone, Black Static, and Orson Scott Card's Intergalactic Medicine Show. Her collections are available in ebook and paperback from Amazon and other online retailers, and links to her published stories can be found at her website: www.transientcactus.co.uk

Paul Edwards is a life-long horror fan and writes his own twisted tales in any spare time that he can grab. He has seen three collections of stories published – *Now That I've Lost You* (Screaming Dreams), *Black Mirrors* (Rainfall Books) and *Night Voices* (Demain Publishing), the latter being a joint-collection with author Frank Duffy. Paul is also a fan of role-playing games, rock music and rough Somerset cider.

Travis Mushanski was born and raised on the Canadian Prairies where he works as a professional brewer in the craft beer industry. He graduated from the BA English program at the University of Regina where he focused on creative writing. Over the past ten years, he's worked as a freelance writer and editor for various online projects. He occasionally finds himself writing short fiction exploring the nightmares and horrors hiding just out of sight. Of course, all of this is possible because of the support of his wonderful wife, Janelle, and beautiful daughter, Emma.

Brian Barnett is the author of the middle grade novellas Graveyard Scavenger Hunt and Chaos at the Carnival. He has over three hundred publishing credits in dozens of magazines and anthologies such as the Lovecraft eZine, Spaceports & Spidersilk, Blood Bound Books, and Scifaikuest.